TH … CTERS

KESRICK, knight of Dragonrouge and our Hero.
PTERON, a friendly sorcerer.
ARIMASPIA, princess of Scythia and our heroine.
GAGLIOFFO, a treacherous Paynim.
AZRAQ, a dangerous Efreet.
ZAZAMANC, an Egyptian wizard and our Villain.
OCTAMASADAS, Arimaspia's wicked step-father.
PIROUETTA, Fairy of the Fountain, Kesrick's Godmother.
MANDRICARDO, a noble knight of Tartary.
MOTHER GOTHEL, a Wicked Witch.
CALLIPYGIA, an Amazon.

Plus:

The Dragon, the Melusine, the Hippogriff, the Rosmarin, the Magic Horse, the Pastinaca, and the celebrated Phoenix.

THE SCENE: Terra Magica, a parallel world whose history has become the source and substance of our myths and epics and legends and fairy-tales.

THE TIME is the twilight of the Golden Age.

. . . Giants and the genii,
Multiplex of wing and eye,
Whose strong obedience broke the sky
When Solomon was King.

—*Matthew Arnold*

KESRICK

Lin Carter

DAW Books, Inc.
Donald A. Wollheim, Publisher

1633 Broadway, New York, N.Y. 10019

Cover art by Keith Stillwagon.

To the undying memory of
James Branch Cabell and
Lord Dunsany, perhaps the
two greatest fantasy writers
of us all.

FIRST PRINTING, NOVEMBER 1982

1 2 3 4 5 6 7 8 9

Contents

Book One
THE KNIGHT OF DRAGONROUGE

Book Two THE PRINCESS OF SCYTHIA

Book Three THE TWO TALISMANS

Book Four: THE FAIRY AND THE WITCH

Book Five THE UNDOING OF ZAZAMANC

BOOK ONE

The Knight of Dragonrouge

I

AT THE WORLD'S EDGE

It had been centuries since last a sound other than the mournful wind had disturbed the stillness that reigned here at the Edge, and at the distant clatter of hooves the Dragon awoke from his slumbers and lay listening.

Hooves meant a horse, and a horse suggested the presence of a rider, and that meant—*Man.*

Man, to members of the dragonish breed such as Dzoraug, meant Food. He opened his left eye, flooding the cavern with crimson light. The gods, who had stationed him here in the Beginning so that he might guard forever the bridge that spanned the starry abyss between this world and the next, had of course seen to it that he should never suffer the pangs of hunger. Just above the mouth of his cave they had planted a curious Dedaim tree, whose undying boughs bore ever a grisly fruit of human heads. To a Dragon there is no tastier a tidbit than Head, hence Dzoraug never went hungry. But the monotony of this diet had, over the ages, somewhat palled on him. He dreamed betimes, and in his dragonish dreams there appeared succulent visions of Arm, or Leg, or even Foot.

Hence that clatter of hooves drawing nearer along the World's Edge, just above his cave, was not a matter of disinterest to Dzoraug. Anything that might alleviate the sameness of his dinner menu aroused his interest; and thus it was that he opened his other eye and peered out of the mouth of his lair and up the steep and narrow path that wound from his doorstep to the brink of the world above.

The unlidding of that second enormous eye increased the sulfurous crimson luminance within the cavern. The light glimmered on heavy rings of gold and on old coins cut with the cartouches of pharaohs forgot ere Nineveh arose, and the names of dynasties extinct save in story. It flashed from heaped and mounded gems in all their scattered thousands—

diamonds and rubies and topazes, pearls and amethysts, emeralds and opals, sapphires and garnets, and on many another gem unknown even to the students of minerals. For the floor of his cavern was carpeted with treasure: gems and crowns and ingots beyond the numbering, and the great Dragon lay sleepily coiled upon this wealth like a mother bird upon her eggs, for a Dragon sleeps not well upon cold stone.

There came to him no further noise of hooves, and Dzoraug wondered if perchance the rider had passed him by, riding north to the Empire of Prester John, or southward, it might be, to Far Cathay, the dominions of the Grand Cham. But he shrewdly guessed that, even now, the rider had dismounted and was looping the reins of his steed about the gnarled and hairy roots of the Dedaim tree, where it leaned over the Edge of the World, and that shortly he would come inching his way down that perilous path that led to his door.

So he waited, did Dzoraug, patiently and also with curiosity. For it had been long and longer still since last there came hither a visitor to his lonely lair at the very limit and margin of Terra Magica (a world which lies as close to our own as do two pages in a book, and of whose histories and geographies our poets and dreamers, tellers-of-tales sometimes glimpse in their deepest dreams).

That last misfortunate visitor had been a Hero . . . what was his name, now? Not Siegfried, surely; something with a "t" in it, thought the Dragon. He could not remember; it had been so very long ago. But the skull and one of the gnawed thigh bones lay in the corner under a heap of coronets.

Great winds howl about the World's Edge, and unless you are very careful they will pluck you from your footing and whirl you shrieking into space, and you will fall and fall and fall forever, for to this abyss there is no bottom, no bottom at all. It is something to think about.

And Kesrick thought very much about it as he climbed, very carefully, down the narrow and steep and perilous stair the gods had cut from the solid rock of the World's Edge, and which led down from the hairy, repulsive roots of that loathsome Dedaim tree to the broad stone doorstep before the mouth of the dragon's lair.

The winds hooted about him, plucking playfully at his locks and tugging at his cloak, which flapped behind him like the wings of some immense bat. It was strange to think that these very winds had arisen first on some far world—Altair, perhaps, or Betelgeuse—but so it was. They had a bitter taste to them, these star-borne winds, the metallic stench of ozone from far nebulae, the sting of phosphorous, perhaps from falling stars, the bitter whiff of thunderbolts.

From here he could see that awesome arch that was the Bridge Between the Worlds, a mighty curve of buttressed stone that soared from the Dragon's front stoop to dwindle from sight among the stars. On that vast road travel the spirits of kings and saints and heroes, en route to the next life.

But the cold winds made his eyes water and the vista of that endless stony arch made him dizzy. He leaned against the world's side and rubbed his eyes, looking down.

Below him, the blue sky purpled into darkness.

Far below him jeweled fires glimmered—stars unknown and as yet unnamed by men.

Beneath his heels there blazed the Southern Cross.

Then a reddish glare fell upon him from the Dragon's staring eyes, and he had come to the bottom of the stair. Here the gods had thoughtfully provided an iron rail for the heroes to brace themselves against as they faced Dzoraug. And he steadied himself against the rail as he hitched his baldric about so that his sheathed sword lay close to hand, yet hidden in the folds of his cloak.

He looked at the Dragon, which all the while regarded him sleepily with two half-lidded eyes like the mouths of furnaces.

The head of Dzoraug was so huge that it completely filled the mouth of his cavernous lair so that he could not come forth therefrom. And the mouth of the cave was itself so vast that you could have built a cathedral therein without scraping a single carven saint or spire against the roof.

Green and mossy with age was that enormous head, grown about with lichens like an ancient boulder, and worn and weathered so that its scales were dull and indistinct.

"Greetings, Man," said Dzoraug in a slow, deep voice that was rusty from disuse. "Are you a hero?"

That question made Kesrick laugh, and his laughter made him forget his fear. "As for that, Great-grandfather," he replied courteously, "we shall have to wait until the end of my adventures to see."

"I mean, are you here on the purpose of heroes? Which is often to slay us of the dragonish race," said Dzoraug.

Kesrick shook his head, red locks tousling. "Nay, Great-grandfather, and when and if I launch upon a monster-slaying career, I venture to say I shall begin with someone more than a bit smaller than yourself."

The Dragon smiled a little at this reply, but suspicion still lurked with him. "Mayhap," he rumbled, "yet I sense about you the tang of magic steel, and is that not a—*sword*—that hangs at your side, poorly concealed under your cloak?"

Kesrick admitted that this was so. "And it is on the matter of swords that I am come hither, for I would beg the answer of a question from you, who are reputed to be the wisest of all created things, as you are rumored to be the oldest."

"Pray step a little closer," suggested the Dragon slyly, "so that we can converse more easily and without raising our voices."

Kesrick grinned and shook his head. "I can hear you quite clearly from here," he said. "And it is never wise to come too close to the jaws of Dragons, even one so polite and hospitable as yourself."

Dzoraug grumbled and shifted his tremendous weight a little. The young knight was well out of reach even of his tongue, which was longer than you would have thought, and was also the means by which he occasionally obtained a meal of Hero.

"Now what would I be knowing of swords?" he inquired a bit peevishly. "They are the ancient bane of my race, and I curse the day the first of them was forged! Chrysaor was its abominable name; Mulciber made it for Jupiter to use in his wars against the Titans. . . . Or was it forged by Hephaestus, for Odin to use against the Frost Giants? I forget much of those days, for my memory is not what it once was. . . ."

The youth felt a touch of awe before such antiquity. "And are you truly old enough to remember the gods, Great-grandfather?"

Dzoraug blinked sleepily. "Young sir, I remember the gods that were before the gods, and the gods that reigned before them. The dynasties of heaven are as numberless as are the dynasties of earth: it is just that they last a bit longer. They all are vanquished by Time in the end, you know, for Time vanquishes all things that ever were, or are, or will be; saving only myself, of course, for the gods that made me saw to it that there should ever be a truce between myself and Time."

Kesrick's green eyes twinkled thoughtfully. He wondered how he could twist the path of their conversation around to the matter on which he had come hither.

"I have heard wise men say that the Dragon Dzoraug

knows everything that there is to know," he said cleverly; "that you crouch here at the World's Edge and dream the slow ages by, and that all knowledge comes your way in the end, when it has been by all the rest of the world forgot."

"I was here at the Beginning and I will be here still, until the End," the Dragon murmured sleepily. His heavy lids were drooping now, closing over the blaze of his mighty eyes like the iron doors of a smithy. He had slept too long to remain awake for long; he was in the habit of sleep.

"I remember the first tree, you know; and the first cloud, for that matter. I am the Oldest Thing there is, for I was the first thing created after the world itself. Ah, and the First Star . . . Oh, but it was very fair! . . . the pattern and prototype of all the stars there are. . . . You do not see stars like that one any more these days."

And Dzoraug fell into a dreamy and contemplative silence—perhaps thinking of that First Star and its supernal and perfect purity and brilliance, as it looked that first of all evenings, when he saw it bloom like a white rose of flame against the virginal skies.

"Yes, I hear much of the world and how it goes, even here where men come not often now," he rumbled drowsily. "The old gods come this way, you know, the tired gods, the half-forgotten gods, on their way to that unthinkable and remote bourn where gods go when men have ceased to worship them, and they begin to fade away. . . ."

"I search for the stolen pommel stone of the sword Dastagerd," the knight said softly. "Perchance you remember it from of old. It is the Sword of Undoings: the Dwarves made it for Dietrich and he slew many monsters with it, before deciding that he liked Nagelring better. The Emperor Huon gave it to Sir Guyon when he knighted him, and Guyon was the ancestor of my house, for I am Sir Kesrick of Dragonrouge."

". . . Dragonrouge?" mumbled the old Worm, more than half asleep.

"Aye. The hall of my fathers rises in a far land to the west, The Kingdom of the Franks. The Red Dragon is my blazonry, and we have been friends, thy brood and my kind, for very long. I thought perchance, when it was stolen away, that it had drifted here to the World's Edge to mingle with your hoard. Oh, tell me, Great-grandfather, if you will and if you can, where might I search for the lost pommel-stone; or, if you in all your wisdom know not, from whom I should inquire of it?"

The great glaring eyes were almost lidded by now, only narrow crescents of scarlet fire showed in the gloom of the cave's mouth.

"There is a sorcerer who dwells in a stone house on the shores of the Isle of Taprobane which lies across the narrow straits from the Kingdom of the Gangarids in Hindoostan," the Dragon mumbled sleepily.

Kesrick listened attentively, and when at last the tale was told, he thanked the Dragon politely and turned and made his slow and careful way back up that steep and perilous stair to where his steed was tethered to the hairy, repulsive roots of the Dedaim tree.

The red luminance had vanished now, and gloom reigned within the vast and treasure-littered cavern. The sleepy eyes had closed and the First of All Dragons slept with his huge snout thrust out over the brink of the bottomless abyss. And it may well be, for aught I know, that as he slept, Dzoraug dreamed, perchance of the world the way it looked on that first morning, green and dewy, fresh and fair.

And that is how it begins.

II

IN THE DUBIOUS WOODS

Through the dark forest Kesrick came riding. The journey from the World's Edge had been long and arduous and his curious steed had grown aweary, as had the young knight.

Weary though he was, he did not pause to rest nor did he care to linger long within the dark aisles of this wood, for this was called the Dubious Wood, and it has never enjoyed the most wholesome of reputations. The silence which reigned about him as he rode was ominous, and the gloom oppressive, for the boughs of the gnarled and ancient trees which grew thickly were yet more thickly intertwined above his head, closing out the sunlight of late afternoon.

Kesrick liked it little; however the way led through the dark, still forest, and the way must be traversed. But this unbroken silence was odd and curious, for in more reputable woods than this there are always tiny creatures scuttling and scurrying through the bushes and the dry leaves, and the chirruping of birds upon the boughs above. In the experience of Kesrick, and in the histories he had read in his youth, forests only fall silent when something large and dangerous and hungry is aprowl.

He rather hoped the histories he had read had been in error on this point, at least.

Across the wide world they had journeyed, his steed and himself, from the remotest Edge across the famous empire of Cathay, and from thence south and ever south they had ventured. Steaming jungles and burning deserts and lakes of liquid fire they had passed and mountains horned with peaks of virginal and untrodden snows, and rushing rivers, and the dominions of quaint and dreadful peoples. From thence they had journeyed down into the many kingdoms of Hindoostan, en route to the Isle of Taprobane.

Thrice had he been forced to defend himself, and had unsheathed mighty Dastagerd in battle: first against a savage and lionlike manticore whom he had encountered amid the mountain snows; a fearful adversary is the manticore, with its long tail armed with a scorpion sting, its triple row of sharklike teeth, its horrible, grinning human face, framed in the uncouth tangles of a matted beard and mane, and its huge body the hot color of cinnabar. But the brute had fled howling from one glimpse of Dastagerd, by which token Kesrick was relieved to discover that even a famous sword long lain unused remains remembered by the monsterfolk.

Later, amid the sweltering jungles, they had chanced upon a rare Tarandus the color of opals. But it, too, had slunk and slithered from the scene, growling in fear. Only the great Ouranabad which had opposed their passage in the Country of the Amazons had given Sir Kesrick a change to bloody his blade: this beast resembles a winged Hydra, and its eating habits are despicable, since it only feeds on writhing and venomous serpents or upon smallish and immature dragons.

That had been a terrific battle, and I can only regret that it has nothing to do with our story, for I would dearly have loved to have been able to describe it for you.

All of these travels and adventurings, to say nothing of the battle against the fearsome ouranabad, had taken their toll of the strength of the youth and of the stamina of his curious steed, so they rode slowly and slower still through the shadows and silences of the Dubious Wood, and at length they came upon a pool of clear water which dreamed serenely under the knitted boughs. And here they must pause to drink.

Kesrick slid from the saddle and undid both bit and bridle, leading his mount to the tranquil pool so that it might drink from the cool, still waters. And he knelt by its side to satisfy his own thirst.

He had not quite fully refreshed himself, when he leapt to his feet in alarm and gave voice to an oath.

For there in the depths of the pond he saw a woman with long floating hair, looking up at him.

He seized the hilt of Dastagerd, then paused, as it were, shamefacedly: for she was slim and young and beautiful, and, also, she was unarmed. And what knight worthy of the name would draw naked steel against a naked woman?

A moment or two later, the Melusine rose to the surface and contemplated him dreamily, floating as light as a leaf on the rippling surface, resting upon her elbows which the water somehow supported. She was slim and young and lovely, in a wistful and languid sort of way, with the slender arms and small, virginal breasts of a maid of thirteen. As Kesrick of Dragonrouge had never before in all of his travels chanced upon one of the Melusinae he may, I think, be forgiven for staring. And, in sooth, she was a rare sight, even in these parts, where mermaids of one or another kind are often seen.

Her body was lucent as cloudy glass so that you could partly see through her; her skin was the palest of blues, almost lilac at the lips and the crisp nipples which tipped her small breasts. But her eyes were like enormous amethysts and her long, silken hair was almost purple. Unlike her sisters of the ocean deeps, she had slim long legs rather than a fish's tail, for she was a fresh-water-dweller.

The watermaid must have realized that she was staring impolitely (although she was staring no harder than was he), for she dropped her eyes and her cheeks were mantled with a maidenly blush of embarrassment, which momentarily rendered them the color of the petals of violets.

"I pray you pardon me, Man, for staring," she said in a thin, faint voice that was like the night-breeze moaning through the reeds that grew at the margins of the pool. "But it has been long and longer still since last I laid mine eyes upon a mortal. . . ."

Kesrick courteously assured the Melusine that he could readily forgive so minor a breach of the proprieties, and spoke up, inquiring as to the route to the abode of the sorcerer Pteron.

At this, her eyes widened again and the watermaid looked a trifle startled.

"Now, I wonder what traffic a mortal knight (and one so fair and seemly!) might have with an aged and decrepit sorcerer who is forever with his nose buried in a fat and greasy book of spells, and his fingers stained with chemicals!" she cried. Kesrick smiled affably.

"Come, come, maid! I have never heard aught concerning the fellow, save that which was goodly; surely, he is not so dreadful an ogre as you describe. . . ."

She smiled shyly, revealing teeth that were not only *pearly*, in the hackneyed phrase of bad poets, but which were, in point of fact, actually pearls. And fresh-water pearls, of course.

He told her something of his quest, and she seemed fascinated by his words, but also just a little apprehensive.

"You risk much by riding through this wood," the mergirl whispered with a sigh. "Terrible creatures dwell hereabouts; in fact, the neighborhood has gone downhill considerably, since I and my sisters first took up our abode in this our lovely pool. Why, betimes I do not feel safe, even in my own grotto!"

Kesrick repressed a smile; the opinion was a common enough one, for every gaffer back in the village of Dragonrouge could oft be heard grumbling that the price of eggs had gone sky-high, the younger people no longer treated their elders with the same sort of respect *they* had treated their elders with when they had been in their long-ago youth, and that the neighborhood (or the village, or sometimes even the kingdom) was going to pot. But he said nothing.

"So you had best be gone from the Dubious Wood, and that as quickly as possible, so as not to be caught herein when night falls," the Melusine counseled him fearfully.

With a quick nod she indicated the direction in which he might find the house of Pteron, and then blew him a shy kiss, and dove to the bottom of the pond with such grace that she caused barely a ripple in the mirrorlike surface of the pool.

Kesrick replaced the bit and bridle and remounted his steed, and they rode on through the darkness and the silence of the Dubious Wood. The young knight could not see the sky, so thickly grown together were the boughs and branches above his head, but his inward sense told him that nightfall was very soon and as all men know, the domain of darkness is the domain of monsters and of Evil.

But now, as a wise precaution, he bore Dastagerd naked in his right hand, for monsters notoriously dislike the tang of naked steel, and even Evil itself does not care very much for it.

This Sword of Undoings, that had ere this hung sheathed at his side, is a brand that goes not unsung in the annals of romance. That famous smith of the dwarves, Brokk—even he, who with his brother Sindri, forged the great ring Draupnir—forged Dastagerd in the fiery heart of the volcano, Mount Aetna; twenty times was the bright blade forged, and twenty times was it melted down and again reforged anew, and each time the smoking steel was plunged into the black and bitter foam of the River Styx for its tempering; and there were dwarf-runes etched along the length of the blade with the slobber of Basilisks that eats like acid, and these were quivering-full of the dark magic of the dwarves, which is as old and grim and full of secrets as are the undermost caverns of the earth itself.

Aye, it was made for Dietrich, and in the glory of his youth he slew many monsters with it: Giants and Ogres, Witches and Lamias, Gryphons and Wyverns, and even Trolls—but never Dragons, for whom the hero had a great fondness, for in his day they were even more of a rare and endangered species than they are today. Not only Dietrich but many other of the heroes of men had swung that bright blade of Dastagerd in battle against men and monsters and magicians, and the name of Dastagerd goes not unforgotten by the makers of song.

And *that* which dwelleth in such ominous and ill-rumored abodes as the Dubious Wood have long, aye, very long memories, indeed, and are unlikely to forget such a sword as Dastagerd. Thus it was that Kesrick was wary but untroubled as he made his slow passage through the dark and silent forest mounted upon his curious steed, although he did not like the silence and the stillness of the leaves.

And ever as he rode he knew that Eyes watched him unswervingly as he passed, Eyes that blinked not, for they had neither lash nor lid; and he knew, or guessed, or at least he *hoped*, that they were Eyes that cared not at all for the light or day, and mayhap even less for the bright shimmer and restless flashing of Dastagerd, which he bore naked in his hand.

But the darkness and the silence, and *that* which watched him with hating but with fearful eyes as he went by, well, those perils were all but behind him now, and in very good time, for night was almost come upon the world, and he would not at all have wished to stray in the wood by night, even with the immortal steel of Dastagerd in his hand.

For by this time he was come at last to the margins of the Dubious Wood, and it was in the very hour of sunfall. And as the gloom and the stillness of the wood fell behind him, the young Frank grinned in relief, which was shared by his steed, for the beast he rode echoed that same sentiment in giving voice to an eloquent but harsh cry, something that was midway between a neigh and a screech, for reasons that shall shortly be made known.

Thus were they come to the shores of the Erythraean Sea, and the house of Pteron lay before them.

And Kesrick was disheartened to discern yet another peril—seven perils, to be accurate—which lay directly between his path and the portal of the sorcerer's house.

III

THE MONSTER-GUARDED GATE

By now well beyond the borders of the Dubious Wood, Sir Kesrick of Dragonrouge reined his restive steed to a halt, and leaned, with mail-clad forearms crossed upon the saddlebrow, thoughtfully contemplating that which lay before him.

The dark waters of the sea foamed against barriers of naked rock, dyed crimson and vermillion by the waning fires of the setting sun. Bleak winds blew, moaning eerily from the shores of Far Cathay, half a world away. A narrow promontory stretched out into the seething waters, and at its ultimate terminus there rose a splendid house, an exquisite villa, built of thirty-seven kinds of marble, of which seven had been known only to the drowned Kings of Atlantis. Roofed with rosy domes was this house, alike unto the domes that crown Shadukiam in the underworld of the Genii. There it soared, the house of Pteron overlooking the moaning billows of the broad Erythraean.

And Kesrick smiled wryly: for the information he had coaxed from the scaly lips of the Grandfather of All Dragons had been, thus far, complete and accurate in all things. For this superb edifice could surely belong to none other than a sorcerer of great power and of perfect taste.

His smile turned just a bit rueful, for, alas!, the Worm Dzoraug had not thought to mention that Pteron's door went not unguarded. . . .

A narrow path led the length of this promontory, between steep and stony precipices; and this road wound betwixt seven high pillars of black basalt. And to each of these was tethered with chains of adamant a Monster.

They lay, or crouched, or coiled, within easy biting distance of whomsoever might foolishly come ariding up that winding way. And by the blaze of their eyes, which glowed through the dusky gloom like so many burning lamps, they were wide awake. And doubtless (he thought to himself) quite hungry, too, since it was not very likely that many travelers would care to visit a house so terribly guarded.

Now Kesrick knew his letters and he conned his Bestiary well, and the dusk was not so dark that he could not clearly perceive the guardians before Pteron's gate. He knew the orange-colored and dragonish Soham from its head, which was shaped like that of a horse, and, of course, the fact that it had quadruple eyes made it all the more recognizable.

The Tregelaphus he knew likewise, for that it was a hideous hybrid, half-stag, half-bull.

And there was no slighest chance of mistaking the Catoblepas for any other monster, when you but pause to consider its long, flabby-looking neck—so feeble-seeming that it is all the Catoblepas can do to lift its ugly head from the ground whereon it usually rests.

And yonder colossal python was doubtless the Askar, he assumed, as no other serpent known to Kesrick's bestiary ever attains the length of sixty cubits.

As for the several remaining monstrosities, yon rather enormous reptile with the sad-eyed human visage, which resembled the Basilisk in all respects save only in its size, was probably a Syl. But the other brutes he could with far less certainty identify. The winged and loudly barking creature with the doglike head might be a Senmurv; the huge, tricephalic monster beyond it could easily pass for a rare Senad, he could not be sure. But these were matters of academic interest merely, and he had practical questions to contend with.

At any rate, the inescapable conclusion to be drawn from this array was that the sorcerer Pteron was inhospitably disposed and took a rather dim view of uninvited guests.

Kesrick grinned mischievously. Then he lightly touched the rowels of his spurs to the flanks of his steed. As he had prudently selected a Hippogriff from the stables to transport him on this venture, it had but to spread its terrific wings to soar easily over the heads of the earth-bound brutes stationed before the gate, to land lightly, and unharmed, at Pteron's door.

The Hippogriff, a hybrid bred by the celebrated wizard Atlantes, one of the most renowned magicians of his day, was a rare blend of horse and Griffin—hence an ideal mount for one whose quest may be expected to span the world. And hence, also, its peculiar cry, half horse's neigh, half Griffin's harsh croaking call, to which I have earlier alluded.

It was the pleasant custom of the sorcerer Pteron to stroll at twilight in his garden, while the spirits who served him prepared the evening meal.

A sorcerer's garden is unlike the gardens of ordinary mortals, as you might assume. Paths of crushed opals wandered between shrubs whose rarity was such that you might have traversed half of the earth without encountering their like. In a pool of brine, a tall pausengi tree grew; it had been taken as a seedling from the true pausengi, which (as the informed reader will know) grows in the salt ocean itself and dies in fresh water. Rarer even than this was the stark white upas that soared in the center of the sorcerer's garden; Pteron had enclosed it under an unbroken dome of transparent crystal, for so deadly is the wood of the Upas if left bare to the ambient vapors of the atmosphere that no human dare come within twelve miles of it on peril of his life.

Hither and thither through the tall grass Baaras roots scurried like hairy and many-footed serpents.

Mandrakes, both bearded and male, and female and plump-breasted squealed and struggled in their loamy beds as the sorcerer approached, uttering sharp, piercing cries, high-pitched and all but inaudible, like the song of bats.

Flowers bloomed as well in Pteron's garden. Their strange, soft petals were of tingaribinus, the Lost Color.

Of such was the sorcerer's garden.

As for the sorcerer himself, he was a lean, sprightly, affable man of elderly and dignified appearance, robed in somber violet and gray. His eyes were cool, deep, and thoughtful; he had a neatly trimmed short beard, sea-green in hue, for his great-grandmother on the paternal side of the family had been a Nag-Kanya, one of the lovely fish-tailed mermaidens of Hindoo lore. He was greatly attached to the sea, perhaps by heredity, and this was the chief reason why he had made his home by its side. Indeed, family legend traced their ancestry back to that very same sea dragon who, in a remote eon, had all but drowned the Buddha (during one of his earlier incarnations as a monkey).

The sorcerer bore on his wrist a most unusual bird, with whom he was deep in conversation. This remarkable fowl, which was about the size of a peacock and no less vivid in its beauty, was the celebrated phoenix itself. A prince of the country of the Gangarids (in which nation Pteron had then resided) had, ages before, given the phoenix to a princess of Babylon of the house of the renowned King Belus of antique memory; even at that remote date it had attained to the remarkable age of nearly twenty-eight thousand years. Upon the collapse of the dynasty, the unusually longevous fowl had returned to the country of its birth, to become a guest of Pteron, with whom it had resided ever since. As the sorcerer was at this time some thirteen thousand years old, the two felt most comfortable with each other, and spent much time together discussing books or personages of date so remote that few else in the world but the two of them had even heard of their names.

At the moment they were quietly conversing together in Chaldean, which, being the earliest of all human languages, was thus the first the phoenix had learnt, and remained the one in which it felt most comfortable. They had been discussing the works of Imlac, the national poet of the Aetheopeans, and had touched upon various of the lost comedies of Epigenes Rhodius, to say nothing of the verses of Astyanassa, a poet the rest of the world has unfortunately allowed to sink into obscurity.

The phoenix had just advanced a quotation from the forgotten works of Sornatius, and the sorcerer was about to top it by a salient reference to the no longer extant works of Calpurnius Bassus, when the great slug-horn which hung at Pteron's gate sounded its clear and echoing note through the hush of twilight.

So well guarded was the road to Pteron's door that it had been some generations since last a traveler had proved himself of sufficient cunning or prowess to live long enough to reach that horn, and thus it was several moments before they recognized it for what it was.

An ornamental balcony was placed above the portal to the marble villa, and therefrom, some minutes later, the sorcerer gazed down with curiosity at the young man who had displayed such temerity as to interrupt his stroll through the twilit garden. He was relieved to discover that the youth had not found it needful to slaughter any of the exceedingly rare and expensive monsters set before his gate, and he examined the uninvited caller with an active and lively curiosity.

This youth (for he was only a year or two past twenty) had a tanned, merry face, an impudent smile, twinkling and mischievous eyes of clear green, and tumbled locks of curly, dark-red hair. He wore a long-sleeved and -skirted chainmail shirt of obviously gnomish workmanship, and over this a loose samite surcoat whose breast bore the emblazonry of a *draco volans*, *gules*, on a field of gray.

The shield, a kite-shaped buckler, also was charged with a red dragon with spread wings which denoted the House of Dragonrouge to every eye learned in the intricacies of the heraldic science.

The phoenix also peered down curiously at the mortal below, as it had been a deal of years since it had last seen a human being (Pteron, with a touch of mermaidenry in his lineage, did not qualify as completely human).

Descrying his signal had at length drawn forth the occupant of the villa, not to mention a peculiar-looking bird, obviously a favorite pet, Kesrick made a nimble leg and smiled engagingly up at the man he had come so far, so very far, to converse with.

"Good evening, Magister! Pray pardon this uninvited intrusion into your privacy, but my mission is of some urgency, and I would discuss with you a matter of mutual interest," he called.

"Young sir, you display a remarkable temerity, if not a laudable tenacity of purpose, in so bearding a magician in his den, so to speak. We who follow the art sorcerous are generally deemed the enemies of ordinary mortals, hence I am surprised that you venture within range of the numerous and malefic spells I possess—any one of which could dash you to the ground speechless, or render you immobile, or strike you to marble in an instant."

Kesrick bowed again, laughing: "I trust in your courtesy, learned sir; and I have never heard the sorcerer Pteron named a villain."

With some asperity, the sorcerer Pteron fixed him with a cool eye.

"By Axieros, Taranis, and Pthah!" he swore, "but you are a confident youth! As for your observation, permit me, in turn, to observe, as the Sage Nectanebus hath remarked, 'Mere abstention from a life of evil does not constitute a life devoted to good works,' from which you might infer that regardless of whatever reputation I may enjoy as not being an enemy of my fellow men, I am not to be considered their friend and gossip, either. Besides which, it was the frequent and deplorable custom of knightly heroes in my younger days, to make their reputation in the world by attempting to dispatch wizards, and suchlike, to their rewards with a swift blow of just such an ensorcelled blade as the one I perceive dangling at your side."

Kesrick cocked his fiery head: "In a word, then, Magister, how do I know that I can trust you not to do me an injury, and how can you be certain that I do not plan to attempt the same to yourself? A dilemma of logic; however. . . ."

They might have discussed their mutual problems of trustworthiness back and forth for quite some time, had not an invisible servant at that moment announced in Pteron's ear that dinner was ready to be served. After thirteen millennia, a man becomes accustomed to eating his dinner at a certain time. Hence Pteron had no recourse but to invite the youthful stranger within his gates, and they all sat down together to enjoy a superb meal, mortal, magician and remarkable fowl.

IV

CONVERSATIONS AT TABLE

The evening meal was served by invisible hands at a long table hewn of ancient oakwood, black with centuries and set with ornate candelabra fashioned from a peculiar metal called hydrargyrum, which the young knight had never seen before or even heard of. The tapers were of corpse-tallow, the most appropriate mode of illumination for one who occasionally dabbled a bit in necromancy.

The repast, whisked out of nothingness by the unseen hands of the servitors, was sumptuous and delicious: there was chopped liver of unicorn served on a bed of succulent herbs from Thessaly, brisket of sea serpent, and a marvelous ragout of steak cut from the flanks of the yale. There were also fresh apricots fetched hither from the Isle of Kirmish and bedded in snow scraped only moments before from the peaks of the Caucasus. And the wine they enjoyed was a precious golden vintage of fabulous antiquity, which they drank from the hollowed horns of the unicorn.

"Superb," said Kesrick after his first sip.

"A rather good year, I agree," commented the sorcerer, pursing his lips judiciously. He could not resist informing his young guest that the wine they were drinking was none other than Imperial Chalibon, the golden wine forbidden to all men and reserved for the pleasure of the Kings of Assyria. Kesrick was suitably impressed, or acted as though he were.

They dined in the Grand Hall of the edifice, a cavernous stone chamber whose walls were hung with tapestries from Hyperborea and weird scroll-paintings from Thibet, which depicted curious divinities with several arms, multiple faces, and the like, enthroned upon enormous coiled serpents, or the backs of fowl, or upon the lotus.

Suspended by a chain of wrought orichalc, a gigantic carbuncle hung from the roof, shedding its gentle and unwavering luminance over the festive scene.

After the meal, they lazed in cushioned chairs drawn up before a fireplace where a tame salamandre lay curled upon a bed of coals, exuding warmth against the chill and damp of the night wind. And they talked, for Pteron was genuinely curious as to what had motivated his knightly guest to beard him in his den. On this subject Kesrick was both voluble and candid.

"But recently my ancestral lands were usurped by a villainous wizard named Zazamanc. It was this personage who thieved away the magic pommel-stone from Dastagerd, thus robbing me of its unique protective powers," the youth began.

"Indeed," mused the sorcerer with some surprise. "I happen to be acquainted with the career of this Zazamanc, from my studies in the histories of the Egyptian magicians. A most renowned archimage, whose powers are commonly deemed as prodigious as is his longevity."

"I remember this Zazamanc well," the phoenix remarked. She had not bothered to join them in their meal, but dined from her customary diet of crushed rubies, served in a golden cup affixed to her perch, which the sorcerer had companionably drawn up to the table. "He was formerly the Grand Vizier of one or another of the Kings of Egypt, either Sosorthos or Sesostris, I forget which."

"Well, as Tarquinius said, 'Lapse of memory is the first sign of old age,' " noted the sorcerer rather sardonically. The fabulous fowl shot him a glance filled with indignation, but did not deign to reply.

"The wizard to whom you refer retired to private practice epochs ago," continued Pteron, taking up again the thread of the youth's tale. "It surprises me that he, who dwells in a subterranean palace in the western parts of Libya, should care to meddle in the affairs of a mere knight, who once troubled the dynasties of emperors and kings."

"He confessed the reason for his usurpation to me during our first and last confrontation," the youth said. "He explained that his horoscope predicted that I and Dastagerd should be the cause of his death, and I presume it occurred to him that my own swift demise would be the simplest and safest means of preventing this occurrence."

"A wise precaution to take, I should say," nodded Pteron. "This Zazamanc is a cautious and prudent man, villain or no. But pray tell me, then, Sir Kesrick, having incurred the enmity of so potent an adversary, how is it that you escaped alive from his, shall we say, clutches?"

Kesrick shrugged offhandedly. "By no heroic exploit of my own doing, Magister, I must confess," he said good-humoredly. "My Fairy Godmother, Dame Pirouetta, rescued me from destruction at the hands of the Egyptian wizard by enveloping me in a cloud which hid me from view, whereupon she instantly transported me to the Pyrénées, where, as you must know, the celebrated enchanter, Atlantes, resides in his famous Iron Castle. It was my godmother who persuaded the enchanter to lend me one of his herd of Hippogriffs, for the breeding of which he is justly famed."

"Indeed," mused Pteron, fingering his sea-green beard. And he quoted an aphorism from the works of Zantipher Magnus in the original Greek, or, if it was not in Greek, at least it was Greek to Kesrick.

"I marvel, Sir Kesrick, that you require the aid of an elderly sorcerer of sedentary habits such as myself, when you have already at hand the capable assistance of a Fairy as powerful as Dame Pirouetta, of whom I have heard much but have as yet not had the pleasure of acquaintance," said Pteron in a questioning tone.

Kesrick sighed. "I fear me that my Fairy Godmother is of the opinion that fairies help those who help themselves," he grinned ruefully. "She was willing enough to rescue me from destruction, and to procure for my travels a magical and tireless steed, and to suggest the wisest course of action which I should, in her estimation, pursue; whereupon she vanished and has since then remained incommunicado—so to speak."

"I see," said Pteron. "Well, now, first let me say that it pleases my heart to discover that some of our older families still respect the ancient traditions. I fear the fine old custom of having Fairy Godmothers has quite gone out of date in these disturbing modern times, and is considered distinctly quaint and old-fashioned. Your ancestors are to be commended, young sir, for their admirable attention to the manner in which these things were conducted in my youth. However, having said that, in all candor, my young friend, I must confess that while I wish you nothing but success in your endeavors to recover your stolen heritage, I have not heretofore been widely noted for my charitable works. In short, sir, why do you expect me to assist you in these adventures, when my natural inclination is to remain here in my comfortable villa, pursuing my scholarly researches in solitude and enjoying the privacy which my advanced years and sorcerous reputation have earned?"

"Because I have not only discovered where the pommel stone is hidden (it is concealed in the enchanted palace of a powerful Efreet on the peak of one of the Rhiphaean Mountains which stand between the most northerly parts of Scythia and the most southerly portions of the country of the Hyperboreans, but that is neither here nor there) . . . and I am afraid that I have lost track of the structure of this sentence and shall have to start my explanation all over again!"

"Then pray begin again, for I am still curious about the matter," urged the sorcerer pleasantly. "However, as the Emperor Fulgentius of Rome puts it, in his admirably terse and succinct style, *'Qui bono?'* " The phrase which sounded elegant indeed in its original Latin, might be translated into the Vulgar tongue, rather bluntly, as "What's in it for me?"

"Also concealed within the palace of this Efreet are many other magical talismans and rarities," said Kesrick smoothly. "And among these may be found the famous Seal of Soliman—"

"An absurd allegation!" snorted the sorcerer with more than a touch of asperity in his tones. "The famous Seal of King Solomon, by which he was able to command the Genii, lies enshrined in the magical museum at Domdaniel, the college for magicians which lies under the seas offshore from Tunis! I have gazed upon it many times in my youth, for it was there I took my first degrees in thaumaturgy—"

"Pardon me, Magister," smiled Kesrick, "but you did not permit me to complete my statement. I did not refer to the famous Seal of Solomon, but to the equally fabulous famous Seal-Ring of Soliman Djinn-ben-Djinn, mightiest of the pre-Adamite kings, he who built the pyramids as well as—"

"I know all about Soliman Djinn-ben-Djinn," snapped Pteron testily. "Including the well-known fact that his ring, one of the most fabulous and potent of all the magical talismans which exist, lies among his treasures at his tomb in the Halls of Ebleez in the Mountain of Kaf; there he reposes, as likewise repose the remains of the seventy-two pre-Adamite kings, and all their talismans and treasures, surrounded by the bodies of their wives, perfectly preserved, who float upon lakes of quicksilver!"

"I very much fear that your information is somewhat out of date, Magister," said Kesrick a bit shortly. "A renegade Efreet named Azraq purloined the Ring of Soliman Djinn-ben-Djinn and bore it away when he fled from the Mountain of Kaf to take up his abode in the enchanted palace atop the Rhiphaeans, to which I have previously referred."

The sorcerer looked stunned. He gazed blankly at the youth, and then a gleam of cupidity flickered in his eyes and he became thoughtful and pensive. For he had not attained to his present, and very considerable, age without having learned to read the character of men, and he sensed beyond question honesty and frankness in the words of this Kesrick of Dragonrouge.

And he very much wished to possess him of the famous Ring.

"Then, in your opinion, we should, as it were, join forces—swordsmanship with sorcery—to burglarize the treasures of the Efreet?" he murmured. Kesrick nodded firmly.

"We will attempt a task that demands not only your own powers of magic, but my small skills with the blade, and such traits of heroism as I may possess," he said.

Pteron looked dubious. "How can we trust each other upon so brief an acquaintance?" he murmured. And then he added, "After all, as Posidippus puts it in one of his most profound dramas," and here he rattled off another Classical maxim. This seemed to be one of his constant habits, and, to tell the truth, it was one that was beginning to become annoying to Kesrick.

"On that point," said Kesrick cleverly, "I can only refer to you the works of the philosopher Zorobasius, in particular to his celebrated treatise on the very subject. His logic, you will agree, is entirely irrefutable!"

"Oh, certainly, certainly," murmured Pteron, who had never in his long life heard of the man, which is not an occasion for surprise, as Kesrick had just invented the name. "But—!"

"And," continued the young knight, overriding him, "To the works of the learned Ptolemopiters, whose arguments on the same question have remained unshaken by generations of lesser critics."

"One of my favorite authors," stammered Pteron, a bit dazedly, "I was reading him just the other night—"

"Then we are in full agreement, of course," said the knight, "and there is nothing more to be said on the matter, save to plan our expedition and to petition the gods for a successful end to the mutual quest."

"Why, yes, I suppose so," mumbled the sorcerer, quite defeated by the citation of these two irrefutable classical authorities.

The phoenix, who said nothing, chuckled wisely to herself.

V

THE MAGIC HORSE

After the conclusion of their meal, Kesrick paid a brief visit to the stables to water and groom his Hippogriff and to see that it had sufficient food and enough clean straw to make its nest (for in their nocturnal habits, the Hippogriffs follow in the habits of their avian, not their equine, components). He then repaired to the house and retired for the night in the sumptuous chamber which Pteron reserved for his very infrequent overnight guests.

As for the sorcerer, he tried to sleep but found his rest disturbed by too many distracting thoughts. At length he rose, and, throwing on a handsome brocade dressing gown, went to his library where he began to reread the *Annals of the Genii*, an old favorite. When even this afforded his troubled mind no solace, he gave it up and went to the room in which he customarily performed his meditations.

It was a somber room, the walls hung with draperies of funereal brown and purple, and, as it had no windows, and thence proffered no views which might distract attention, was perfectly appointed for the purposes to which Pteron put it.

Now there is a certain charm or cantrip known only to the saintliest of the Brachmans, and originally disclosed to mankind in a revelation from Brachma himself, by means of which the soul may easily be detached from the body to roam the universe with complete mobility and freedom, traveling with the speed of thought.

This charm, which the Brachmans call "the Mandiran," was well known to the sorcerer, who had employed it many times in the past. He had learned the secret from Prince Sikandar of Balassor, which is one of the multitudinous kingdoms of Hindoostan, as devious and clever a villain as ever there was, who had obtained the secret by bribing one who possessed it with the treasures of Golconda. The charm was remarkably simple, and, once learned, cannot be eradicated from the memory.

Pteron repeated it now and instantly his spirit departed from its place of residence. With knowledge of the Mandiran, this is as simple to accomplish as it is for you or me to slip out of our garments. The empty body, a mere shell, thereupon falls into a dreamful trance while the soul voyages as it will.

The soul of Pteron, then, having achieved the upper atmosphere, traversed the breadth of the world, arriving within instants at those mountains where the youth had claimed might be discovered the palace of the Efreet. To one side of these foreboding mountains lay the land of the Hyperboreans; to the other, the grassy plains of Scythia, with the Rhiphaeans standing betwixt the twain like a wall built by the Genii to divide the nations.

The palace of the Efreet was concealed from the eyes of mortals by a wall of illusion which rendered it invisible, but such illusions have no power to impede the clarity of vision enjoyed by the bodiless spirits, hence Pteron found it erelong. It rose on the crest of the very last mountain in the range, which fronted upon the shores of the Frozen Sea, and it was a magnificent structure, adorned with precious stones, ornamented with windowframes of pure silver, and even the gutters on the roofs were of solid gold.

The unimpedable vision of spirits has another unique faculty, in that it can detect the aura of power surrounding holy relics or enchanted talismans. Hence the spirit of the sorcerer soon discovered that both the missing pommel stone of Dastagerd and the famous Ring of Soliman Djinn-ben-Djinn were present within the edifice. This greatly relieved his mind, for only a fowler by profession cares to pursue the wild goose, and Pteron would have loathed having his studies interrupted by a vain quest, such as the one he was soon to embark on in the company of Kesrick.

Having satisfied himself that the young knight had spoken nothing but the truth, the sorcerer's spirit traversed the span of the world once again, and reentered its vacant vessel, which stirred and woke and, its worries allayed, soon found the calm repose earlier denied it.

With dawn, over a huge breakfast involving thirteen different kinds of jam and steaming omelettes made from the eggs of the ibis, the sorcerer reiterated his nocturnal discoveries and the two resolved to depart at once for the borders of Scythia.

Pteron packed wicker baskets with various implements of the Art Sorcerous which he deemed it likely he would later need, and also loaded them with a copious supply of provender, as adventurers often find their perils and exploits tend to lead to a ravenous appetite.

"Pardon me, Magister," said the youth tentatively, "but I am not at all certain that the pinions of my Hippogriff will prove strong enough to support the creature in midair, burdened with my weight and your own, and so much baggage."

The sorcerer smiled, for he was in rare good humor this morning, and he affably explained that there would be no reason for all of their luggage and themselves to burden the poor creature, as he possessed an aerial contrivance of his own. As Kesrick expressed polite curiosity on the nature of the vehicle, Pteron led him to the stables and proudly drew forth from the stall next to the one in which the Hippogriff lay curled in its nest a steed, if anything, even more marvelous than Kesrick's own.

It looked entirely like a horse, but it was inanimate, a thing fashioned from gleaming ebony. Its hooves were shod with plates of red gold and it was caparisoned in the most splendid fashion imaginable. It was, in fact, no less famous a magical treasure than the celebrated mechanical flying horse of the Kings of Persia, once the proud possession of Prince Camarelacmar.

The sorcerer produced a golden key with which he wound the clockwork creature up, and soon it was cavorting and tossing its wooden head for all the world as if it were a living beast and not a clever magical contrivance. Kesrick could scarcely believe his eyes, but, after all, this *was* Terra Magica, where marvels and wonders are as commonplace as pebbles and mud puddles are in our mundane world.

Pteron pointed out the knobs which controlled the Magic Horse in its flight, and how easily one could adjust the height, velocity and direction of its celestial canterings. This concluded, they loaded the baskets upon the withers of the Magic Horse and prepared for their departure. Pteron and the young knight bade the phoenix their farewells, and, warmly cloaked against the cold winds of the upper atmosphere, mounted their steeds.

In less time than it would take me to describe it, they had left the earth below and were soaring through the winds of heaven. It was a marvel to Kesrick that the horse could fly without wings, and it amused his sense of the ridiculous that its maker had designed its inner works so that as it flew weightless as a leaf it imitated the galloping motions a horse makes as it races on the ground.

The two flew directly north across the hills and vales and jungles of Hindoostan, pausing only briefly to admire the celebrated beauties of the Vale of Cachmir and the famous gardens of the Shalimar, which, at this clement season, were in full and gorgeous bloom. Then they veered west a trifle, in order to avoid the Himalayas, and headed for Scythia.

It was not possible for them to converse during their long and wearying flight, for the Hippogriff had a wingspread of thirty feet, and they must either fly in tandem or separated by a considerable space. This being the case, to exchange words they would have had to shout rather loudly, but, even then, the winds which roared and shrieked about them would have snatched the words away the very moment they had left the lips of their speakers, so perforce they remained silent. But as they soared above interesting sights or places, the sorcerer would catch Kesrick's attention and point to the object to which he wished to draw his companion's attention. Among these were the ruins of Babylon, still encircled by the towering height of its immemorial wall, the Imgur-Bel, which was still accounted among the seventeen wonders of the world, amid whose sprawling wreckage still loomed like a man-made mountain the legendary Tower of Babel, built by King Nimrod.

They soared above the Caspians and the sorcerer drew to the attention of the young knight the famous rampart of shining brass built anciently by the Divine Alexander to hold at bay the savage tribes of Gog and Magog, which peoples still were safely penned up behind the mighty barrier and were helpless to break free and overrun the world, which they certainly would have done long since, were things otherwise.

And they flew over the great Kingdom of Persia, admiring, from their unique point of vantage, the spires and domes and minarets of Susa and a host of other splendid cities that flashed and sparkled in the bright morning sun as if fashioned entirely of polished gems and the noblest of metals.

As they ventured farther and farther north, of course, and left the sunny kingdoms of the south behind them in their flight, the scenery became less hospitable. They flew above the dark, stormy waters of the Caspian, and the empty plains of Scythia, and the sky darkened and the clouds gathered, turgid and lowering and of the color of iron.

Directly ahead of them, on the far horizon of the world, there came gradually into view a grim and gloomy range of great mountains which marched for a time beside the narrowing straits that led from the upper Caspian to mingle with the icy waters of the Frozen Sea. Beyond that range, which was none other than the Rhiphaean, Kesrick knew, lay the country of the mysterious Hyperboreans, and, even farther to the west, the Ocean Sea itself, amid which a traveler would find the little known island of Ultima Thule.

But our travelers, of course, were not traveling in that direction at all, but to the northernmost peak of the range, whereupon the terrible Efreet resided in his enchanted palace of gold and jewels.

When they had come within sight of the peak, Kesrick, of course, saw nothing but flat stone and empty air, but according to the vehement gestures of the sorcerer, they had apparently arrived at their destination. Such was the strength of the tireless wings of the Hippogriff, and the potency of the enchantments which animated the Magic Horse, that they had achieved their goal and it was not even yet noontime.

Kesrick leaned over and murmured praise in the ear of his steed and stroked the fine fur which clothed its strong shoulders. I have not yet had occasion to describe the Hippogriff, but it was smaller, more slender and considerably lighter of body than the usual destriers ridden by knights errant, and very much smaller and lighter than the ponderous stallions ridden in tourney. In color it was a handsome roan, with magnificent wings feathered the hue of new bronze, and the very tips of the feathers were edged with the brightest gold.

It resembled a horse in every respect, save in its mighty wings, its beaked Gryphonlike head, its clawed feet, and in the fact that its head bore a stiff crest of bronze feathers, rather than the usual mane of hair. Such was the Hippogriff; the knight called it "Brigadore," for that had been the name of the noble steed ridden by his famous ancestor, Sir Guyon.

And even at that moment, Brigadore did that which brings him as an actor into our narrative, for, chancing to espy a strange sight far beneath his feet, the Hippogriff threw back his head and gave vent to that strange cry, half-neigh, half-squawk, to which I have elsewhere alluded.

Kesrick leaned over in the saddle, searching the bleak and

rocky shore beneath them, where cold waves of black water broke in flying spray, striving to ascertain the cause of the Hippogriff's consternation. And at the sight which met his astounded eyes, he at once drove his steed into a spiral decline, and rapidly descended toward the surface of the earth.

Completely mystified, the sorcerer watched him descend. "O, Aglibol, Tarku and Centeotl!" he swore, using the names of divinities so obscure that it is to be doubted that, even had the youth been close enough to hear his ejaculation, he would have ever heard of them. "Whatever has gotten into the lad *now?*" he groaned.

But there was nothing to do but descend to earth himself, and discover what had caught the attention of the youth.

BOOK TWO

The Princess of Scythia

VI

A DAMSEL IN DISTRESS

Descending to the foot of this northernmost mountain of the Rhiphaeans, Kesrick of Dragonrouge saw more clearly what he had glimpsed from above when alerted by the cry of his Hippogriff, Brigadore. It was a beautiful maiden.

She was chained to a great rock, which affronted upon the Boreal main, with shackles of rusty iron. Kesrick sprang from the saddle as soon as his mount had alighted, and examined the bound maiden with an attentive and very interested eye, and in truth she was well worth looking over.

Her head was crowned with a magnificent mane of long hair which fell below her narrow waist, for all that she was tall and slender, and as graceful as are the dancing girls of Cachemir. Her hair, by the way, was like the palest and purest gold, and caught the fitful gleams of sunlight through the turgid clouds above as if composed of strands of the finest silk.

Her enormous eyes were the rare shade of violet sported by amethysts, and were fringed with the longest lashes Kesrick had ever seen. And her flesh was as if molded from pure cream, and completely without blemish, at least insofar as Kesrick could see, and since the maiden was as naked as on the day of her birth, he could see virtually everything that there was to see, and everywhere his eyes roamed they feasted on nothing less than complete loveliness.

He was enchanted to discover that her full and luscious lips—which were the color of rose-petals—precisely matched in shade and hue the rosy peaks which crowned her nude and perfect breasts.

For her part, the maiden saw a handsome and stalwart knight in glittering mail, upon a fantastic winged steed. He was only a very few years older than she was, for she had just turned sixteen, and she thought him remarkably attractive.

The young woman, who had just been uttering a fervent prayer for rescue from the sea god of her people, one Thamimasadas by name, regarded him with wide incredulous eyes.

"Fair sir," she cried above the thundering of the noisy surf, which broke about her bare and (Kesrick could not help noticing) splendidly turned ankles, "are you come, like the Chevalier Rogero upon your winged steed, to rescue yet another Princess Angelica from that sea monster, the Orc?"

The historical parallel had not, of course, escaped the notice of Kesrick, who was delighted by it. But yet another similarity had occurred to him, as he was quite well read in history.

"Nay, madame," he replied, making a leg, "but as another, and lesser, Sir Perseus to rescue from a more fearsome doom a far lovelier Andromeda!"

The maiden blushed at this beautifully phrased compliment, and Kesrick was enchanted to note how the rose color spread from her cheeks to mantle her naked breast, throat and even her shoulders.

"Then perchance, sir," she said, "like another Chevalier Bellerophon, mounted on a more agile Pegasus, you will battle against a yet more fearsome Chimera, to save—"

At that moment, as things would have it, something huge and monstrously ugly breached the waves considerably offshore, as if in order to reconnoiter the strand, and the young woman broke off with a fearful cry.

"Pray let us postpone our discussion of the historical precedents to another time," said Kesrick, and he unlimbered Dastagerd and advanced to free the beautiful young woman. It took but a stroke or two of his enchanted steel to sever the rust-gnawed iron of her shackles, and within moments she was free.

"I am hight Sir Kesrick of Dragonrouge," he introduced himself. "A knight errant of the Franks, bound upon a quest but proud to be diverted in order to be of service to one so fair and in such dreadful peril. But tell me, if you will, madame, what fiend has bound you here to perish from the inclement elements of this hostile clime?"

"I am Arimaspia, a Princess of the Royal House of the Scythians," she replied. "For some time a ferocious monster from the deeps called the Rosmarin has been ravaging the coasts of our kingdom, and my royal parents have in vain dispatched eleven champions to destroy the beast, but all have ended up in its gullet. Whereupon my wicked stepfather, King Octamasadas, third of that name, persuaded my weak-willed mother, Queen Thomyris, to revive an ancient custom for appeasing the wrath, or the lust, of such monsters, by binding to this bleak rock the most beautiful of the virgins to be found within our borders."

"Of which yourself, obviously, were the first unfortunate to be chosen," said Kesrick gallantly, feasting his eyes upon her loveliness. She smiled at the compliment, dimpling her rosy cheeks in the most delightful manner imaginable.

"Actually, Sir Kesrick, three of my younger sisters went first, I fear, to satisfy one or another of the appetites of the Rosmarin," the Princess of Scythia confessed.

"I can hardly deem it credible," murmured Kesrick, quite fascinated, "that even the famous Kingdom of Scythia could boast of daughters more fair than the beauteous Arimaspia!"

At this moment, the Rosmarin chose to break the surface of the frigid ocean again, and it could be perceived that his enormous bulk had come very much closer to the shore upon which these two young people stood.

"Permit me to assist you to mount my steed, and we shall be gone from this place as swiftly as we may," urged Kesrick, offering the naked Princess the warmth of his cloak, which she disdained as, being a true Scythian, she was more than accustomed to the climate.

"Nay, sir knight," cried Arimaspia, "for that would but inflict yet further sufferings upon my people! Like another Angelica, I await to observe my hero dispatch to his doom a vaster and more ugly Orc!"

Kesrick inwardly groaned, for he could have wished to have avoided the contest, but chivalry bade him obey the pleas of the Princess.

By this time, of course, the sorcerer Pteron had descended upon his Magic Horse, and was introduced to the Scythian Princess, who acknowledged his greeting with a regal, if distracted, nod; to tell the truth, she could hardly take her eyes from the handsome and manly person of Kesrick of Dragonrouge, who found himself equally unable to divert his gaze, even momentarily, from her nude loveliness. Pteron, who had observed these adolescent passions many times before, and who was, of course, very long past them himself, groaned inwardly and repeated to himself a maxim from the writings of

Quinapalus which ran to the effect that how swiftly the hungers of the heart can divert even the noblest-minded of heroes from the most exalted of quests.

Just then, that monstrous head broke the seething waters of the boreal main, and this time our adventurers could observe it more clearly. The head alone, slick and streaming with water, was bigger than a bull, and the eyes were immense globes of canary-yellow fire, burning with unmentionable appetites and utterly devoid of the finer sentiments, such as those which surged high in the knightly breast of Kesrick, who stood with his arm wrapped protectively about the bare shoulders of the Princess Arimaspia, whose full and naked breasts were, a bit uncomfortably, pressed against his suit of Gnomish mail. Not that she voiced any objection, of course. . . .

The Rosmarin, spying the tender girlflesh which had been royally proffered to sate whatever lusts or appetites he might have enjoyed the satisfaction of, and espying as well the two unexpected strangers who stood near her, gave voice to a choked and gurgling roar of fury, blubbery lips peeling back from enormous fangs the length of cavalry sabres, and hurtled toward the shore with all the velocity his huge flippers could attain. And now it could be seen that the body of the monster would have dwarfed the most prodigious of whales.

"Go, my knight and champion," cried Arimaspia, flinging her bare arms about the neck of her savior and bestowing upon him a kiss which made his lips tingle, "and defend the right of Arimaspia to live, and to reward you suitably!"

The young knight, whose imagination ran riot with speculations as to the precise mode and form and nature of the reward the naked girl promised him (for these Scythians were not generally considered to accept the more prudish morals of his own westerly realm), cast a desperate eye upon the sorcerer. But Pteron, heartily annoyed at the interruption of chivalry into their nefarious enterprise, afforded him no offer of assistance.

"Yes, hasten, Sir Hero, to dispatch the monster!" Pteron said smugly. "We shall await your safe and victorious return somewhat farther up the beach, in order to avoid the splatterings of blood."

Well, there was nothing else for Kesrick of Dragonrouge to do but to put a bold front upon it, although he inwardly quaked. As the elderly sorcerer gallantly offered the Princess of Scythia his arm and assisted her up the strand and well out of harm's way.

"Princess, may I offer you the warmth of my cloak?" he inquired solicitously, but she impatiently declined.

"This is no time to bother about such fripperies!" Arimaspia exclaimed, "Not while yon noble knight stands in peril of his mortal life, bravely facing the monstrous Rosmarin!"

Pteron did not bother to press the point, and the two watched as Kesrick sprang astride Brigadore and ascended into the winds.

The Rosmarin, which by this time had clambered clumsily into the shallows and was wallowing amid the sucking tides, proved even more enormous than it had at first appeared to be, and much uglier, if possible. It was the color of raw liver, and with its slick, wet hide somewhat resembled the sea lion or the walrus, although it was larger than a thousand put together. As well, a fiendish intelligence burned in its goggling and sulfurous eyes, an intelligence far beyond the cunning of beasts.

It now craned its neckless head skyward, tusks gnashing together like boulders in a maelstrom, observing the Frankish knight as he swooped and hovered on his winged steed. It did not at all enjoy the sight of Dastagerd, which the hero bore naked in his right hand.

With the beautiful young Scythian Princess looking on in trepidant adoration, there was nothing at all for Kesrick to do but to assume the mantle of a hero. Thus, brandishing his ensorcelled blade, and uttering in a clear, ringing voice the ancient motto of his house, he fell to battle with the Rosmarin.

"*Comite ferro!*"* cried the young knight, aiming a vicious blow at the immense and blubbery monster, which unfortunately missed.

In the very next instant, the Rosmarin had knocked him from the saddle of the Hippogriff with a well-timed swipe of its huge flippers, and the astounded knight found himself in the surf, soaked to the skin, gargling cold salt water, with the monster looming above him.

* Or, "The sword is my companion."

VII

THE MONSTER FROM THE SEA

Rising spluttering from the shallows, Kesrick bravely strode deeper into the boiling surf and engaged the Rosmarin in battle. The receding tide sucked at his feet and dragged at his knees, making his stance uncertain and putting him at a distinct disadvantage in the conflict; on the other hand, the immense, blubbery Rosmarin was in the shallows, which put the monster also at a disadvantage, so perhaps the disadvantages were equal.

He hewed lustily, dealing mighty strokes with his enchanted sword, but naught seemed to disincline the Rosmarin from the contest. The irresistible steel of Dastagerd sheared away slabs and chunks of Rosmarin meat, but none of these injuries seemed to give the maritime monster the slightest pause. Although blood flew in every direction and turned the churning surf to carmine, the monster continued its attack with unabated vigor, seemingly tireless, its clashing jaws coming ever closer and closer to the knight's flesh, guarded though it was behind a longcoat of mail.

Far up the strand, well beyond the reach of the hungry surf, Arimaspia and the sorcerer Pteron watched the battle closely. The Scythian Princess, in an agony of apprehension, clasped her hands in the warm valley between her perfect breasts, breathing prayers to Thamimasadas, and to any other divinity of the Scythian pantheon who might be amenable to her beseechings.

Pteron, who stood protectively at her side, and who observed the conflict no less closely than did the Princess, stood, of course, prepared to intervene with his magical powers at any instant when he deemed the young knight to be in deadly peril of his life, for the sorcerer had conceived of a considerable and avuncular affection for this Kesrick of Dragonrouge, and would not stand idly by and contemplate with tranquility his destruction; nonetheless, he was determined to permit the Hero ample opportunity to demonstrate his prowess without the aid of the Art Sorcerous.

Kesrick, in the meantime, now soaked to the very skin in icy waters, puffing and blowing like a walrus, was engaged in beating back the ferocious Rosmarin. Although with every stroke of Dastagerd he sheared away slabs of blubbery flesh, reeking with hot gore which stained the roiling waters, he soon discovered that none of his mightiest strokes so much as slowed the tireless monster. True, it bellowed wrathfully at every slice, but continued to press forward with bared and slavering fangs, not in the least bothered by the several pounds of meat which Kesrick had thus far removed from its huge and rotund shape.

But, just as Kesrick was faltering and on the very verge of falling back toward the beach, there occurred one of those chance accidents which are the delight, as they are often the salvation, of the authors of mere fiction.

For, apparently having gathered its strength from the distance of the Boreal Pole itself, there came at that instant driving in toward the northern shores of the continent, a billow of such height and weight and of such tremendous and irresistible force, as to knock Kesrick off his feet; but, fortunately, it was of such force that it drove the Rosmarin, helplessly squalling and flopping its flippers, high upon the shore.

And on the dry land, obviously, the monster was virtually helpless. For, as the mighty wave receded into the bosom of the deep, and as Kesrick came wading grimly up the slope toward the sandy place where the monster roared and wallowed, helpless to move its enormous bulk (which, all the while, steamed with slimy gore from many wounds inflicted upon its person by Dastagerd), the knight wearily, but with immense satisfaction, perceived that his dreadful adversary was rendered helpless and thoroughly indefensible.

Farther up the strand, in the shelter of the rocks, the Princess of Scythia, wringing her white hands desperately, uttered a fervent prayer of thanksgiving to her gods, while Pteron breathed a sigh of relief, glad that he did not have cause to intervene in this shining moment of heroism and monster-fighting to rescue his young protégé.

"Even with such puissance did Sir Rogero slaughter the dreadful Orc, to effect the rescue of the beautiful Princess Angelica!" breathed Princess Arimaspia, her perfect, and very naked, breasts heaving with every panting breath she took, her limpid eyes shining with adoration.

Pteron, who had called the riderless Hippogriff to him with a piercing whistle, now tethered the beast to a stunted pine which grew between the rocks, and turned to smile cynically at the maiden. With the measure of his advanced age he was long past any of the passions of the flesh, save perhaps for the pleasures of a well-spread table or a bottle of excellent vintage, therefore he viewed her tumultuously heaving bosom unmoved.

"Quite likely so, Highness," he remarked. Although urged to do so from his malicious humor, he refrained from pointing out to the maiden that it had been a chance billow of unusual strength that had bestowed the laurels of victory upon the brows of her handsome hero, rather than any noteworthy prowess of his own. But, then, he was a gentleman, born and bred, and tact was, as he himself often observed, his specialty.

As they watched, an exhausted Kesrick of Dragonrouge dragged himself, soaking wet and chilled to the bone, out of the squalling surf and began to clamber up the prostrate bulk of the stranded monstrosity. Such was the size of the beached Rosmarin, that it took the knight some considerable time to ascend its girth to the point at which he imagined its heart to be, providing, of course, that such hideous creatures possess the organ.

He poised the point of his blade above the breast of the recumbent Rosmarin, and was about to plunge it home with the last of his depleted vigor, when not only Sir Kesrick, but the Princess Arimaspia and even the sorcerer Pteron were frozen with amazement to hear the sea monster utter an imprecation in a deep, slobbering tone, but nonetheless in distinctly human language.

"Slay me not, O Brother of Lions, for I am the most unfortunate of the servants of heaven, being imprisoned within the body of this hideous monster and unable, for such are the weaknesses of the flesh, to oppose the dictates of its furies and of its loathsome and despicable appetites!"

Kesrick was petrified with astonishment, but soon recovered, nor did the point of his ensorcelled blade for one instant waver from its position above the vital organ of the Rosmarin.

"Vile monstrosity," he declared in ringing, if slightly

breathless, tones, "dare you attempt to evade the just punishment of your innumerable crimes against humankind by means of prevarication and subterfuge? Know that the enchanted steel of Dastagerd, Sword of Undoings, is poised at this instant to sever the bonds of life, and to plunge your atrocious spirit into the depths of that Lake of Fire which a merciful and omniscient Providence has created for the purging of such beings as yourself!"

"Eloquently spoken!" breathed Pteron to himself; for, as an old connoisseur of the heroic sentiments, he admired nothing quite so fully as a well-turned and polished phrase. The Princess, whose eyes were aglow with admiration, shot him an indignant glance of reproof, and he fell silent, this being not entirely his scene, as yet.

The prostrate Rosmarin goggled its bulging eyes up at the grim face of the young knight who stood athwart its breast, and stared into his face with an appeal nigh irresistible to such chivalric souls as that which burned with the breast of Kesrick.

"I am naught but a lowly miscreant," groaned the monster, "transformed by enchantment into this hideous and bestial form which now lies helpless before your steel! But hear me out, O Fountain of Hospitality, and, if I may, I may yet persuade you that a human heart beats within this ghastly corse!"

It was then that the sorcerer strode forth to where the young knight of Dragonrouge stood panting and dripping astride the recumbent monster.

"A word, Sir Kesrick, if I may!" said the sorcerer, lifting one hand. "It is not given, of nature, for such monsters as yonder Rosmarin to possess the divine gift of articulate speech! I must presume, therefore, that something of what the creature says we may assume to be the truth; that is, that it is in sooth an unfortunate mortal transmogrified by the Art Sorcerous into the likeness of a monster. And in this case, as chivalric gentlemen, we should, at very least, listen to the protestations of the loathsome creature, before dispatching it to whatever horrid punishment Providence hath reserved for it and its like!"

"Very well, then," sighed Kesrick, every limb aching with fatigue and shivering with cold from the icy winds which blew upon his sopping-wet body. "I will permit the Rosmarin to explain its predicament, while reserving judgment until we have heard the monster out. Speak on, malformed lump of loathsomeness, for we will hear you out, at very least, for the code of chivalry demands nothing less from its exponents!"

Turning its goggling eyes upon them, the Rosmarin thereupon addressed his audience in deep, hoarse, and croaking tones, as follows:

"I was not always as you see me now, for once I was one Gaglioffo, a Paynim, born in the westernmost parts of Libya, beyond the Moghreb. Life, my masters (and beauteous mistress) is hard for one so misfortunate as to be born devoid of grace, prowess, beauty, wealth, or noble birth; we unfortunate ones born devoid of these, the noblest gifts of heaven, must perforce find a living as we may, hence it was that I, in my poverty, turned to the burglaring profession, and attempted, in the hugeness of my heart, to redistribute the wealth of the World from the very rich to the very poor, among the which I venture to name myself, Gaglioffo."

"Continue, unfortunate soul," bade the sorcerer.

"Finding myself unaccountably in the northern parts of the World," continued the Rosmarin, "I entered into the country of the Hyperboreans, and, hearing of the inordinate riches possessed by one Abaris, repaired at once to his abode. He was then, as I was given to understand, absent upon a world-spanning mission, gathering wisdom from among the savants and sages of many distant realms. I had but just entered his palatial residence, and had chosen but a few gewgaws and trinkets wherewith to lighten the burthen of mine poverty, when this very Abaris unexpectedly returned, finding me, as one might say, in the very act!"

"Ah," murmured the Magister interestedly. "Pray continue in your discourse."

"The estimable Abaris, most uncharitably, viewed my purloining of a few superfluous treasures in the direst of attitudes," groaned the Rosmarin. "And, in short, transformed me into a sea-monster as you see me now, and flung me into the depths of the Frozen Sea, to fare as best I might. My informants," the monster added ruefully, "had not seen fit to explain to me that Abaris was a powerful enchanter, or I might well have seriously reconsidered my thieving schemes."

"I recall this Hyperborean," murmured Pteron to the young knight; "we were schoolboys together at Domdaniel; he was always jealous of his possessions, and I recall me well one time I wished to borrow his Arthame, but he would not lend it me. A selfish and proud fellow, by Aipolos, Merodach and Tuisco!"

"By Zaqqum, the Tree of Hell, and by the Well of Zamzam, but I have been prisoned in this grisly form long enough!" wept the unfortunate Gaglioffo. "I pray you, Sovereign of the Age and King of Time, of your sorcerous art, to free me from this accursed flesh, permitting me to attire my soul once again in the swart but comely form in which Dame Nature at birth ornamented me!"

The sorcerer was not insensitive to the Rosmarin's plight, and as both Sir Kesrick of Dragonrouge and the Princess Arimaspia of Scythia begged him to accede to the request, the sorcerer, somewhat reluctantly, determined to try.

"The misfortunate fellow is little more than a mean burglar and a vile rogue," declared the sorcerer virtuously, and somehow managing to ignore the fact that he himself was present upon the scene for thieving motives, "but, if you two will indeed have it so, I will attempt to disenchant the monster with whatever poor skills my mine Art affords."

At these welcome words, the Rosmarin lay back with a hoarse groan of relief, and called upon the Mighty Mahoum to succor it in the extremity of its need, and to lend his miraculous aid to the thaumaturgical powers of the sorcerer.

Seating herself daintily upon a boulder, the Scythian Princess looked on with keen interest, for she had never before in her sixteen years of life witnessed a disenchantment.

VIII

DISENCHANTING GAGLIOFFO

While Sir Kesrick held the helpless Rosmarin at bay with the keen point of Dastagerd against the monster's breast, the sorcerer Pteron bustled over to where the Magic Horse stood patiently awaiting the next command of its master, and began rummaging through the wicker baskets slung across the ebony withers of his ensorcelled steed, muttering absentmindedly under his breath.

"Now let me see," the sorcerer muttered to himself as he rummaged, "powdered mandrake root, dried wing of bat, pickled eye of newt . . . hm, hm! . . . wherever did I put that magic wand? I remember tucking the dratted thing in here somewhere—ah, there we are! Now, what else, what else . . ."

Erelong he had found the various instruments and ingredients required for the operation of magic, and came down the beach to where the monstrous Rosmarin lay on its back, goggling hopefully over one shoulder at him, with Kesrick still astride its breast.

"We shall have you back in your proper shape in the proverbial jiffy, my good fellow," the sorcerer assured it in brisk and businesslike terms. Kesrick and Arimaspia, who were fascinated at the prospect of witnessing a disenchantment, seated themselves upon nearby boulders in order to overlook the spectacle.

Pteron produced several bottles, flasks and tin boxes of powders from his wicker baskets and mixed the contents of these together, tossing the finished potion down the open throat of the recumbent monster. Having imbibed of the concoction, it could be seen that the monster promptly fell into a deep and seemingly dreamless sleep.

Thereupon, the sorcerer next built a small fire from a dry bundle of pungent-smelling herbs, and seated himself upon the sands, legs folded beneath him tailor fashion. Once the small fire was burning brightly, with tall, licking tongues of flame shooting up, he scattered upon the blaze a handful of powder from a small box; instantly, the flames produced a thick coil of violet mist, which was as richly fragrant as the most odorous of incenses.

This mist gathered about the heaving bulk of the helpless Rosmarin like a cloud, concealing its hideous body from their view. Pteron then began intoning the rhythmical words of a magical verse, spoken in a language none of them had ever heard before, while bending his lean body back and forth over the blaze, as if drinking in the strangely colored smoke.

"Fascinating!" breathed Arimaspia to the knight in low tones.

"And very instructive," he whispered in reply.

The chanting voice ceased; the incantation, or de-incantation, now seemed completed. They waited with breathless anticipation for the final revelation.

The sorcerer bowed once more over the flames of his miniature bonfire, which had died to glowing coals. Then he climbed, somewhat stiffly, for his joints ached from the clammy sea air, to his feet, and stood regarding the cloud-shrouded form, which appeared to have shrunk noticeably in size.

He flung his arms above his head in a ritual gesture.

"Yeowa!" he cried in a loud, commanding voice.

The violet cloud swirled—boiled—seethed—contracted—then dissipated.

Where the huge body of the Rosmarin had lain there now sprawled on his back the body of a Paynim!

He was black as soot, and even uglier than the Rosmarin had been, with thick, blubbery lips, goggling eyes, now squeezed tightly shut, a fat wobbling paunch and bowed legs. He was naked to the waist, save for an open vest of red felt, and his lower limbs were covered with voluminous pantaloons, gathered tightly about the ankles. A gaudy sash was tied about his belly and red slippers with up-curling toes were upon his feet. His head was crowned with a huge tarboosh of crimson stuff, and gold hoops bobbled in his ears.

He seemed to be a Moor, as far as they could tell.

"Open your eyes," commanded Pteron. The Paynim did so, staring about fearfully. Then he glanced down at his ugly body with every expression registering delight; hugging himself ecstatically, the Paynim rolled over the wet sand, ending between the feet of the sorcerer which he covered with blubbering, happy kisses.

"O Sovereign of Time, O King of the Age!" the Paynim crooned in tones of delight.

"Have I, in sooth, restored you to your true form?" inquired the sorcerer. Nodding his head so violently that the motion threatened at any moment to dislodge his tall tarboosh, the sooty Paynim indicated that it was so.

"Very good, then," said Pteron, a slight smile of satisfaction visible upon his features. "I've never used a de-incantation before, and am delighted to learn that it resulted satisfactorily!" Packing up his bottles and herbs and powders, he replaced these in the wicker panniers slung across the ebony hindquarters of the Magic Horse, while Gaglioffo crouched on the sand before the Frankish knight and the Scythian Princess, trying to cover their feet with slobbering kisses, which Kesrick endured as best he could, while the Princess withdrew her bare feet disdainfully.

"Filthy creature, you would have devoured me!" she cried in disgust. At which the Paynim nodded humbly.

"Yes, Queen of Blossoms, or even worse! As was the case (Mahoum forgive me!) with your delectable three sisters—"

"Come!" said Pteron commandingly, "the past is the past, let us forget it and turn to present matters. Both yourself, despicable Paynim, and Sir Kesrick there, are soaked to the skin. Let us repair to the upper ground, seek shelter, warm ourselves before a fire, and perhaps enjoy a spot of lunch, before proceeding to the fulfillment of our quest!"

They soon found a niche in the rocky flanks of the mountain, which protected them from the sea wind, and Gaglioffo scrambled about in a servile manner, gathering fallen branches and dead leaves from the few stunted and twisted trees which grew about the base of the mountain.

When these had been piled in a shallow pit Kesrick had dug in the sand, the sorcerer touched them alight with a Word which invoked one of the elemental spirits of Fire, and before long a cheerful blaze was merrily crackling and the four were gratefully warming themselves by its light.

Kesrick stripped off his surcoat, which had been soaked in the boiling surf, and wrung it out and then draped it over a rock facing the fire so that it might dry, while Arimaspia helped the sorcerer unpack lunch from the wicker baskets, which viands they spread out upon a dry cloth stretched out over the sand in the manner of a tablecloth.

"By Golfarin, the Nephew of Mahoum, but you are a powerful magician!" exclaimed Gaglioffo some few moments later, chewing hungrily on a chicken sandwich.

"I have some little skill," admitted the sorcerer modestly, dipping into a tasty paté and sampling an excellent dry white wine.

Gobbling down a ripe peach and tossing a slice of ham after it as if to keep the peach company in his gullet, the Paynim exclaimed: "All that the miserable Gaglioffo has had to eat for days and days and days was an occasional virgin, not to mention a champion or two." He gave a slight belch. "Champions give me gas, O my masters!" he added.

Arimaspia inquired of the Magister if the transformation would prove permanent, or would Gaglioffo have to worry about turning back into a Rosmarin again.

"Gaglioffo is now returned to his true and natural form," Pteron said, nibbling a bit of brie. "Such as it is, of course," he added. "Therefore he will remain as he is unless someone transforms him in the future into something else—"

"Which Termagant Herself forbid!" groaned the Paynim in fervent tones, knuckling his low forehead in obeisance.

"But he would be wise to stay out of Hyperborea," suggested Pteron, "since my colleague Abaris has a long memory."

Gaglioffo nodded vigorously, and although he said nothing, one might correctly have assumed that the Paynim's personal philosophy might well have been summed up in the phrase, Trust in Mahound: but tie up your camel.

The wind had died, although still the skies of early afternoon were hidden behind turbulent and leaden vapors. In mid-nibble upon a pomegranate, the Princess fell asleep, her golden head pillowed upon Kesrick's thigh. It would seem that the terrors of the long day had worn out the Scythian maiden, but his own exertions and perils had wearied Kesrick as well, and he nodded off, his red head pillowed uncomfortably against a boulder.

The sorcerer let them rest awhile, as he and the famished Gaglioffo finished off the remnants of the meal. Regarding the sooty Paynim with a certain scholarly curiosity, Pteron inquired of him as follows.

"What was it like, being imprisoned in the body of a monster?"

The Paynim shuddered, hugging himself.

"The depths of the sea, O my master, are cold and dark and lonely," said Gaglioffo in a hushed voice.

"And wet, as well, I should expect."

"Oh, very wet, Source of Wisdom!" wailed Gaglioffo. "Naught was there to eat but flounder, haddock, herring, and the occasional whale," he added soulfully. "How this unfortunate Paynim used to yearn for the taste of toasted cheese, or ripe olives, or an apricot!"

"I can imagine," murmured Pteron, not unsympathetically. "Any change of that diet must have been earnestly desired."

"Indeed so, O Wiser than Solomon!" sighed the Paynim, licking his thick lips reminiscently, perhaps remembering the virgins.

Then he inquired of Pteron as to the reason which had brought the sorcerer and the Frankish knight into these extreme and northerly parts.

"—Unless it was merely to rescue yet another virgin, of course," added the Paynim as if by way of an afterthought. Pteron frowned.

"No, we had not the slightest notion of the perils in which Princess Arimaspia recently found herself," the sorcerer admitted. And then in a few terse, well-chosen phrases, he informed Gaglioffo of the quest upon which he and Sir Kesrick were bound. The Paynim shivered upon learning that his rescuers were about to beard a powerful Genie in his den, so to speak, and asked for what possible reason they wished to place themselves in such deadly danger.

Perhaps prudently, however, Pteron refrained from telling him about the two talismans. He could not have quite explained the reasons for his reticence upon this point to you at the time, had you been present to ask.

Shortly, thereafter, both Sir Kesrick and the Princess Arimaspia awoke from their brief but refreshing nap, and fell to upon the remains of their luncheon—those few scraps which the hungry Paynim had left undevoured, that is. Pteron broached another bottle of the excellent white wine of Kismische, keeping in reserve a bottle of the red wine of Schiraz, at which Gaglioffo was gazing thirstily, with many lickings of his pointed red tongue about his blubbery purple lips.

"We shall keep back a few scraps, and a drop or two, for later," murmured the sorcerer prudently. "After all, who can say just how long this adventure will last?"

IX

THE ENCHANTED PALACE

By the time they had completed their repast, Pteron was anxious to depart, for all during the luncheon he had been glancing nervously at the heavens, as if striving to ascertain from the position of the sun the hour of the day. But, as the sky was all grim and turgid, the horizon black and ominous, with great volumes of writhing vapor obscuring the view and lit, ever and anon, by the red flickerings of vivid lightning, glimpses of that luminary were brief and fitful.

"I quite agree that we have naught to gain by loitering any further upon this bleak and hostile strand," said Kesrick, "but I must confess that I am puzzled as to the cause of the urgency I sense in your tones, Magister."

"It is quite simply explained," declared the sorcerer. "You may have been a bit surprised at the precipitate haste with which we departed this morning from my residence; had it not been for certain matters which I have yet to impart to you, I should otherwise have taken at least a day or two in making my preparations for this adventure. But last night, having ascertained to my satisfaction that the talismans we seek are indeed among the treasures of the palace above us on the mountain peak, I took the simple and prudent precaution of looking up what is known of the history of this particular Efreet in a volume from my library, the celebrated *Annals of the Genii*; therein I found an ample section on our huge friend, whose name happens to be Azraq the Blue. I discovered that it is also the immemorial custom of this Efreet, on this very day, that is to say, today, to leave untenanted his palace atop the high Rhiphaeans to pay his annual visit to his brother, a Marid called Akhdar the Green, who dwells beyond the deserts of Libya, in the Mountains of the Moon."

Kesrick's green eyes twinkled mischievously. "I begin to

understand!" he exclaimed. "I had, of course, wondered by what clever plan or subterfuge you expected to gain entry to the palace of so powerful a spirit; it had not occurred to me that the safest and easiest way would be to effect our entrance during the absence of the Efreet. That being the case, let us mount and begone without further delay, for I greatly fear that all of these rescuings and disenchantments (to say nothing of that delicious lunch) have consumed more time than we may comfortably afford, and that the greater part of the day is already gone."

They then mounted their respective steeds, Sir Kesrick taking the Scythian Princess before him in his capacious saddle, while the sorcerer, with some little expression of distaste, allowed the Paynim to clamber up behind him. A touch of the reins, a turning of the knob, and the two flying steeds ascended to the mountain's ultimate crest.

To the gaze of all, the peak seemed merely to be a flat and empty plateau devoid of the slightest trace of habitation; but, as this was obviously the result of that magical barrier of illusion to which Pteron had earlier referred, they led their steeds across the vacant and wind-swept plateau until suddenly the palace of the Efreet appeared before them, melting into being, as it were, out of empty air.

"Oh!" exclaimed the Princess, clapping one exquisite hand to her no-less-exquisite lips in astonishment and delight. And Kesrick experienced much the same emotions, for the palace was built on a scale of magnificence as to beggar comparison with any other structure the youth had heretofore seen. It was crowned with prodigious spires and minarets which soared into the lowering clouds, and behind these swelled the enormous rondures of domes which resembled the full moon in their shining splendor.

The gates of the palace, which stood directly before them, were built on a scale of such magnitude that they would have easily afforded an entry to Giants, had any of that breed been so foolhardy as to have ventured the attempt.

This frowning bastion, which soared higher than the tallest of trees, presented an unbroken barrier of glistening brass, and written upon its frontal was the following inscription, set down in the queer, rude characters of the language of the Genii, which Pteron could easily decipher and translated for them as follows:

It is no light task to disclose the portal of this asylum:
The bolt, rash passenger, is not of iron, but the tooth of a furious dragon:
Know thou, that no one can break this charm
Till Destiny shall have consign'd the key to his adven-t'rous hand.

Having listened to the rolling syllables of this enigmatic quatrain, Kesrick and Arimaspia pondered its gloomy implications with furrowed brow. Gaglioffo shuddered at the import of the mysterious message.

"*Wullahy*, my masters!" wailed the Paynim, "and since we cannot enter the dreadful palace by the front door, then let us yield over this venture and depart at once for a more hospitable clime!"

"Nonsense," scoffed the sorcerer, unperturbed. "It is quite true that we cannot force the portal, but there are always other means of entering."

"Instruct us, then, of your wisdom, O Reader of the Planets!" whined Gaglioffo. The sorcerer shrugged and pointed aloft, where vast casements stood ajar.

"If you cannot go in by the door, you can always try one of the windows," he remarked. They remounted and soared into the interior of a hall so vast, in its extent and height, as to resemble a stupendous chasm.

"Sir sorcerer," the Princess addressed Pteron, "it puzzles me that this Efreet should have barred his portal with spells of such efficacy that even your skills cannot undo them, but left his window open."

Pteron smiled. "The Genii possess prodigious strength and command impressive powers, it is true; but they are very simple-minded, easily befooled by clever men who manage to keep their wits about them, and have the intellects of little children. Now come, let us secure our steeds and begin the search."

Kesrick tethered the Hippogriff to a great bronze ring set in the nearer wall, and, hand in hand with Arimaspia, they followed the sorcerer as he strode purposefully toward the middle of the hall, with Gaglioffo scampering fearfully behind.

The roof of this hall, which was so far above them that small white clouds drifted in and out through the clerestory windows, was supported by titanic pillars of malachite huger than stony sequoia. The walls themselves were entirely covered with painted portraits of impressive bearded monarchs or patriarchs, which Pteron informed them represented the seventy-two pre-Adamite kings who had ruled the dominions of the world before the creation of men, and among the which, of course, was painted the enthroned figure of the redoubtable Soliman Djinn-ben-Djinn himself, with the huge gold Seal-Ring on his finger.

After a good hour, or somewhat more, they had reached the portal which led to the interior chambers, and passed through it, trying to ignore the grisly veil which covered the entrance, and which consisted of glistening eyeballs of lions, tigers and bears, threaded upon strands of scarlet silk.

Beyond, they found themselves in a chamber built somewhat more to their own proportions, and this room was strewn with the most incredible profusion of wealth as to bring instantly to the goggling eyes of Gaglioffo the gleam of purest greed. His gnarled fingers twitched as he surveyed the tempting treasures, but a severe glance from the sorcerer caused him to wilt and to restrain his burglarious appetites.

In brief, the floor of this chamber was heaped with lion skins fetched from Mount Atlas, and ingots of shining silver, and bars of Numidian copper, and elephant tusks from the Makkar, and thick bundles of peacock plumes. The air was rendered fragrant by aromatic hanging lamps of perforated brass, and the luminance of the burning lamps fell on heaps of sea-green smaragdites, lodestones from Hyperborea, and red carbuncles condensed from the urine of lynxes.

Kegs and casks and flagons bore a wealth of rare spices and condiments, citron, thyme, basil, powdered jessamine, frankincense, gum storax, rosewater from Fajhum, and narcotic powders from Aracan. In short, the chamber contained sufficient treasure to purchase the ransom of a satrap.

But nowhere did the keen eyes of the sorcerer Pteron discern either the pommel-stone of Dastagerd or the ring they sought.

"Let us pass on," he said curtly.

They entered a second chamber, larger than the first, where huge crocks stood, filled to the brim with coins of gold and silver stamped with the bearded visages of Kings of Phrygia or Paphlagonia, and any number of Seleucids or Ptolemies. At this appetizing sight, the eyes of poor Gaglioffo virtually bulged from their sockets, and he would have eagerly stuffed handfuls of this coinage into his baggy pantaloons had not, once again, the Magister bent upon him a stern warning glance.

"It was my understanding that you had already surveyed the Efreet's palace in spiritual form, by means of that Mandiran spell of yours," Kesrick spoke up bewilderedly. "Why, then, are we wasting time searching room after room of this interminable palace, when you should be able to lead us to the talismans direct?"

"I did not enter the palace, Sir Kesrick," Pteron informed him in distracted tones, "but merely ascertained by their aurae that the two talismans were within. We shall have to find them with patience, I fear—"

"Magister," said Arimaspia, "why cannot you once again liberate your soul by means of this cantrip you possess, detecting once more by their aurae their position within the palace, and then, returning to your proper fleshly habitation, lead us to the hiding place forthwith?"

It seemed to Kesrick and Gaglioffo a sensible proposition, yet was the sorcerer understandably reluctant to leave his bodily shell empty and unprotected, against the imminence of the Efreet's return, which he expected to momentarily occur.

Explaining this to his companions, he added, "I should rather wait until all else has failed before resorting to so drastic a mode of discovery. Let us move along!"

They passed, thereupon, through chambers and suites and apartments, corridors and rotundas and hallways, littered and bestrewn with fabulous treasures. There were great heaps of inestimable pearls, the stacked horns of unicorns, glowing carpets of Persian-work and tapestries of fabulous worth from Hindoostan and the Isles of China, goblets and dishes of wrought gold and silver, strange idols of jade and malachite fetched from Java and Borneo and Soccotra, but nowhere did they discover the lost pommel-stone of Dastagerd, or the Ring of Soliman, Djinn-ben-Djinn.

They were almost at the point of giving up in despair, when suddenly they came upon a portal which led into a vast open enclosure, roofed by the mightiest of domes. And an expression of enormous relief lightened the gloomy features of the sorcerer.

"By Agathodaemon, Zababa and Latobius!" he exclaimed, "but I do recognize the position of this enormous dome as that within which the talismans were concealed!"

"And about time, too," grumbled the Moor under his breath.

They hastened to open the bronze portal and rushed eagerly within, only to stop dead in the next instant to stare about them in amazement and consternation.

For in this enormous room it would be utterly impossible to discover the talismans, for reasons which shall shortly be made known to you. . . .

X

THE GARDEN OF JEWELS

The vast dome was built all of rosy quartz and through its lucency vagrant shafts of sunlight diffused in a pink hazy glowing, by which light they could discern the spectacle which lay before them.

Here the Efreet had contrived a fantastic garden of precious stones and noble metals. Gnarled and quaintly twisted trees of silver or bronze bore up crowns of branches wherefrom hung leaves made of wafer-thin slices of jade, and blossoms carved from amber, topaz and tourmaline. Globed fruit hung on golden wires from some of the amazing trees, fruit fashioned from polished but uncut rubies, sapphires and emeralds.

Vines of finely wrought gold sported grape leaves cut from plates of malachite, wherefrom dangled bunches of ripe grapes made of amethyst and black opals.

Between the trees of this garden grew what appeared to be a velvety lawn; upon closer examination, it proved to be composed of slivers of dark jade, wherein sprouted toadstools carven from tiger's-eye, cinnabar or carnelian.

Everywhere that their dazed eyes wandered, their vision drank in such a profusion of rare and precious and even semi-precious stones, that the treasury of Croesus seemed niggardly in comparison. Everything that was within the enchanted garden aped Nature, but everything was cunningly fashioned from minerals.

Quartz and agate, porcelain and crystal, sapphires and lapis lazuli, ivory and electrum, zircons and alexandrites, porphyry and enamels, chrysolite and mother-of-pearl . . . the wealth of vast empires and sultanates lay strewn about them, beggaring the fabled treasures of Ormuz and of Ind.

They looked farther, beyond the blaze of jewels.

Here and there about the fantastic garden, streams meandered—but not streams of water, no, nor even streams of wine: instead, but shallow troughs through which tumbled opals, moonstones, and pearls in similitude to the transparent fluid.

Paths meandered here and there about the garden, but they were not paved with gravel. Instead, lumps and chunks and morsels of pure gold composed their lengths.

In the center of the garden, a fountain stood; all of pure rock-crystal was the bowl thereof, and from the vent cut diamonds spouted, flashing, into the air to clatter in the crystal bowl.

Here and there about the garden, perched upon the bronze or silver or golden boughs, mechanical Bird-of-Paradise, flamingoes, ibis or nightingales, fashioned with cunning artifice from precious metals, their feathers blazing with gems, flapped their wings and uttered melodious, if mechanical, song.

It was, the astounded travelers were forced to agree, a remarkable sight. But, also, it was depressing.

"We could each of us search this garden for a year," groaned Kesrick, "without finding, in all this profusion of gems, the talismans we seek!"

"I fear me you have hit upon the truth," Pteron sighed.

Gaglioffo could hardly believe his protuberant and sooty ears.

"Oh my masters," he implored, "what else is there in all of the wide world to seek for, with such wealth lying all about us unguarded? Come, let us fill our pockets and begone, and once free from this uncanny palace, we can each purchase emirates or princedoms!"

They paid the greedy fellow no attention, each busied with his or her own grim thoughts.

"The Genii are remarkably stupid, as a race," murmured the sorcerer. "But what better way to hide two magical talismans, than among acres of gold and gems? This Azraq obviously is possessed of a certain amount of low, brutish cunning. Well, there is nothing else for us to do but return to the Grand Hall, and employ the Mandiran, Melcarth aid me!"

He led them all beyond the entrance of the garden into the outer hall and there sought and soon found a small, secluded alcove where he could be alone with his meditations. Sternly bidding them not to disturb his body while it slumbered untenanted, he closed the door and knelt tailor fashion upon a priceless Isfahan carpet, and recited the Brahmin spell.

In the hall beyond, Kesrick was pacing restlessly to and fro, while the Princess was admiring her reflection in a mirror of burnished silver. Gaglioffo huddled miserably in a corner with his head in his hands, groaning dolefully and thinking of Treasure.

"How long, Sir Knight, do you think that it will take the sorcerer to locate the gems you seek?" Arimaspia inquired.

"Not long, I think," said he.

"And then we will be gone from this palace, I trust?"

"As soon as can possibly be managed," he affirmed. "Whereupon, I believe we should first return you to the bosom of your family, who will doubtless be relieved to learn that you are safe and that Rosmarin had been, if not slain, at least done away with."

Her cheeks dimpled in a provocative smile that sent the pulses of the young knight racing.

"My wicked stepfather," she said demurely, "has offered the hand of one of the royal Princesses in marriage to any hero or champion fortunate enough to destroy the scourge of the sea monster."

"Is that the truth, then?" murmured Kesrick. Their eyes met in a long, deep exchange of glances.

His eyes glistened, and she smiled. "A mere formality, of course," the Princess added, "for certainly my wicked stepfather never expected me to be rescued; but, you must admit, in the fine old tradition of the way these things were done in better days, even as St. George rescued the Princess Sabra from the Dragon, and was granted her hand."

"Is it really true?" murmured the knight. "And doubtless a huge treasure, to boot?"

"Oh, goodness, yes! *Sacks* of rubies!" said Arimaspia (which made the eyes of Gaglioffo glisten).

The eyes of the knight and the maiden met in a long, eloquent, unspoken exchange of thought, but, as to what may have passed at that moment through their minds, or, for that matter, through their hearts, I will not venture to say.

The sorcerer had led them back into the vast front hall of the palace, where small clouds still wandered to and fro high up near the roof. And, even as the lovers—for, surely, that is what they were by this point!—continued staring dreamily into the depths of each other's eyes, there occurred an untimely interruption.

Thunder rolled, like ten thousand kettle drums.

Lightning blazed, fiery yellow and fierce crimson.

A jet-black storm cloud rolled before the enormous door, spreading the stench of sulfur and brimstone which stung the nostrils and made them gasp.

And the Efreet appeared.

He was taller than the tallest pine, and uglier than imagination can depict. His prodigious strength was evident from the massive thews which swelled across his deep chest, his broad and sloping shoulders, and his long, apelike arms, whose hands were armed with hooked talons as long as the scythes of harvesters.

His round glaring eyes were like balls of yellow fire and his thick lips, peeled back in a grimace of evil glee, bared fangs like the tusks of elephants.

Gold hoops the size of carriage wheels dangled in the lobes of his pointed ears, and coarse hair fell across his shoulders from a topknot on the back of his skull, writhing like black serpents.

Thick bands of heavy iron clasped his wrists and ankles; a loincloth made of seven hundred square yards of red cloth hung about his waist; a triple necklace of tiger skulls clanked about his thick throat.

He was altogether hideous.

Such was Azraq the Blue; and moreover, he was well-named, for his hide was the color of indigo and his forked tongue was purple.

The Genie bent his fierce gaze upon the tiny humans that cowered between his feet, neither of them coming any higher than his ankle.

In one hand he brandished an immense scimitar of shining steel, a weapon so huge that it could easily have cloven an Alp in twain at a stroke.

"So," he boomed, his voice like thunder, "there be thieves in my house! Thieves and vile burglars, I warrant, by Kashkash!"

Kesrick thrust the Princess behind him and stepped forward manfully, Dastagerd naked in his fist, but his heart quailed within his breast, for steel alone could not vanquish the giant Efreet, and with a sinking heart he knew himself helpless.

Once freed of its fleshly abode, the spirit of the sorcerer Pteron drifted through the walls of the great hall, traversed again the chambers bestrewn with treasure, and entered for a second time into the domed Garden of Jewels.

Everything that greeted his vision was exactly as it had appeared to the eyes of his flesh, with the exception that by the subtler senses of the spirit he could observe, here and there about the bewildering expanse of gold and jeweled trees, the flickering aura of magical objects.

There were quite a few of these within the Garden of Jewels, but he did not pause to ascertain their nature, searching instead for the pommel-stone, which he soon found, and the Ring of Soliman Djinn-ben-Djinn.

Once he had clearly marked and memorized the position of the two talismans so that he would be able to locate them without difficulty, once he had returned to his body, the spirit of the sorcerer left the Garden of Jewels and traveled back to the little alcove where he had left behind him his clay.

"How can you hope to engage such a ferocious giant in battle, my knight?" whispered the Princess Arimaspia in a faint, forlorn voice. "He could combat elephants or tigers with his bare hands; how, then, can any hero, even one who goes armed with an enchanted sword, dream of vanquishing the brute?"

"Where courage can't suffice to win the day," breathed Kesrick between his teeth, "then wit alone must enter in the fray."

And with those bold, or perhaps despairing words, the young knight of Dragonrouge stepped forward and lifted a hand to catch the attention of the Efreet, bending above them like a bettling cliff.

"One moment, sir!" he called in a ringing voice. "Methinks from your words that you do be suffering from a misapprehension!"

Azraq the Blue, who had just lifted one bare, clawed foot the size of an iceberg to crush them underfoot as a man might step on bothersome insects, paused to eye the minuscule figure inquiringly.

"Eh?" he rumbled, the huge foot still hovering in mid-air.

And Kesrick smiled briefly, for in the extremity of his need he had chanced to recall something that the sorcerer Pteron had remarked a bit earlier.

BOOK THREE

The Two Talismans

XI

THE GENIE APPEARS

The gigantic Efreet bent from the waist in order to regard the minuscule human figure that confronted him.

"What is it that you have to say, mortal?" he demanded in a voice like rolling thunder.

Kesrick was thinking rapidly; indeed, more rapidly than he had ever thought before. And he put a bold front on things, there being nothing else to do.

"You are quite correct, Sir Genie," he shouted, "in your suppostion that vile thieves and despicable burglars are on their way to rob you of your treasures!"

"I know as much, Mortal, for already have I caught them in the very act," roared the Genie, bending above him like the frowning battlements of some enormous structure built by giants.

Sir Kesrick glanced swiftly about him: the nude Princess of Scythia cowered against the wall, her amethystine eyes huge and fearful; Gaglioffo, had crawled shudderingly beneath a heap of Persian carpets; the untenanted body of the sorcerer Pteron was well concealed in the alcove he had selected for its privacy. Kesrick again addressed the towering monster.

"But you are mistaken!" he yelled. "For we are not the thieves you seek; I am Sir Kesrick of Dragonrouge, the heir of an ancient and noble house of the Frankish kingdoms, and this maiden is the Lady Arimaspia, Princess of the royal house of the Scythians. Surely, you, who partake of the spiritual, can read our hearts and souls, and will realize that between us we command great wealth, and are hardly likely to burglarize the palace of one of the mightiest of all the Efreets!"

The ferocious visage of Azraq expressed now the look of

bafflement. "Then why are you here!" he demanded, rather reasonably.

"Why, indeed!" shouted the young knight accusingly. "We, who have ever been friends to the Genii; we, who have never been the foes or enemies of your kind; why, think you, sir, we are come?"

The Efreet looked puzzled, burning eyes rolling widely. "I do not know," he rumbled slowly, in a voice so deep that it caused their very bones to ache.

"Because, being apprised by a friendly sorcerer, now absent, that vile enchanters sought to rifle your treasures, O Azraq, and ever having been faithful friends to the Genii, we came hither on the flying steeds you observe yonder to frighten them away, to rescue your treasures from these burglars, and to give you warning of what was about to commence!"

The Efreet looked, if anything, vaguely flattered.

"That was very nice of you, mortal," he rumbled.

"Fortunately," said Kesrick, his voice getting just a bit hoarse from all this shouting, "we seem to have arrived just before the coming-hence of the villains who would rob you of your choicest treasures! Therefore, Sir Azraq, might I suggest that you ascend into the upper atmosphere (as my sorcerous friend apprises me that the burglars will be arriving by air), in order to guard the approaches of your magnificent palace, while we, already on the scene, will conceal ourselves from view, and await to confront the thieves, should they not be intercepted by yourself!"

"But—!"

"Hasten!" shrilled the young knight, his voice breaking. "The moment of their arrival is almost to hand! Do you wish to be robbed of the rarest treasures you possess?"

"Not at all," rumbled the Efreet.

"Then do as I beseech you—ascend into the upper heavens, and survey all arrivals carefully, while we lurk hidden hereabouts in order to surprise your enemies in the very act of stealing your finest and rarest possessions!" urged Kesrick.

The Genie complied: a rolling cloud, bristling with fiery thunderbolts, gathered about his towering form, which dissolved into its primal substance. In a moment of two (save for the whiff of sulfur and brimstone), his giant form had vanished, and Kesrick collapsed, breathing heavily, into the angle of the wall.

The Princess, similarly exhausted from nervous tension, sagged against him and covered his face with breathless kisses, such was her admiration for his feat of persiflage and cunning.

"I did not really lie to the huge creature, you know," he said when he came up, however briefly, for air. "Thieves are active about the premises, eager to filch some of his treasures; they are arriving (or have recently arrived) by air; and neither you nor I have, I trust, ever done aught to offend the Genii."

"My hero!" she breathed, and was kissing him again. Well, before long, one thing led to another, as is often the case, and hands wandered to explore less familiar terrain, and matters were rather well along, given the hot blood of the young people, when the Magister appeared on the scene, freshly attired in his bodily vestments once again.

He put his hands on his hips and surveyed the two youngsters with pursed lips and a disapproving eye.

"I have no idea—" he began in severe tones, at which sudden interruption the two came suddenly apart, breathing heavily, and looking rather flustered; "I have no idea," he continued, "what fevers may boil the blood of youth, but, surely, the two of you could find a more appropriate scene and point of time to conduct these furtive amours, since I expect the return of the Efreet Azraq at any moment."

Kesrick adjusted his somewhat disheveled clothing guiltily, avoiding the sorcerer's reproving gaze, while Arimaspia adjusted her flowing mane of sungold hair. "Actually, Magister," said Kesrick, panting for breath, "all is quite nicely taken care of in that department."

"Oh?" said the sorcerer inquiringly, elevating his brow.

"Indeed, Sir Sorcerer," said the Scythian Princess, "just before your precipitous arrival upon the scene, Kesrick encountered the Efreet (as dreadful a monstrosity as ever I hope to see!) and deluded him with carefully chosen and artfully phrased half-truths."

"Did he, indeed!" said Pteron, marveling.

"I but remembered me your very words, Magister," said the young knight, "to the effect that they are simple-witted fellows, for all of their prodigious size and strength, and as easily cozened as children."

"Well, then," huffed the sorcerer, somewhat mollified. "But where is Azraq at this moment?"

Kesrick grinned and gestured overhead.

"Somewhere in the vicinity of the Boreal Star, for all I know or care," he chuckled. "Eagerly vigilant to watch the approach of vile aerial burglars, of whose ominous plans I apprised him!"

"Well, then, by Acoran, Qat, and Abraxas!" swore Pteron feelingly, "let us get to work, for there is no telling how long your prevarications, skillful and persuasive though they doubtless were, will detain the Efreet! And where is that rogue, Gaglioffo?"

"Skulking under yonder carpets," sniffed Arimaspia. The Paynim was soon roused from his hiding place by a few well-placed lusty kicks, and the three adventurers quickly retraced their steps, reentering again the domed enclosure where lay the Garden of Jewels.

The Princess regarded the sorcerer curiously.

"And did this Mandirain spell of yours enable you to locate the talismans which are, I am given to understand, the object of your dual Quest?" she inquired.

The sorcerer smiled with satisfaction. "On the matter of the hiding place of the gems," he said confidently, "I am inerrant. Behold, my Lady of Scythia!"

And without faltering, Pteron strode to a cluster of pale jade grapes: groping behind them and untwisting a small golden wire, he produced in his palm the long-lost pommel-stone of Dastagerd, the Sword of Undoings, over which Sir Kesrick uttered crooning exclamations.

Pteron then proceeded to stroll rapidly down one of the garden paths, until he reached a spot at which he paused, bent, searched among the golden gravel at his feet with questing fingers, and rose to display with pride a mighty annulus of shining gold so huge it might have clasped the biceps of a Hercules.

"Feast your eyes upon the celebrated Seal-Ring of Soliman Djinn-ben-Djinn, master of all the Genii!" he proclaimed.

Gaglioffo plucked at his sleeve.

"And now, perhaps, O Brother of Lions," breathed the faint-hearted Paynim, "may we not begone from this fearful palace of many perils before the befooled Efreet returns to devour our very bowels in his rage?"

"Vilely phrased," sniffed the sorcerer, not deigning to give him a glance, "but the sentiments thereof I can only approve!"

They repaired again to the great hall, whereupon they

resumed flying mounts, and once again, while Kesrick took before him in the saddle the naked Princess of Scythia, Pteron perforce must offer a place behind him to the ugly heathen. And, in less time than it would take your chronicler to describe the action, they had soared through the huge and open casement and found themselves buffetted by the winds of heaven, high above the peak of the mountain.

The sun was even now expiring on a crimson bed in the west, and the sky was heavily charged with a tumult of vapors which seethed in the throes of conceiving a storm. So furious were the howling winds that there was no conversation possible between the riders of the two aerial steeds, but Kesrick caught the eye of the sorcerer and gestured vehemently to the east. With an inward sigh, Pteron reined his ebony steed in the direction in which the Hippogriff was even at that moment hurtling, and followed his young friend through the airs of heaven.

They flew for some period of time, all of them anxious to put as much distance between themselves and the Efreet Azraq as could be afforded; over the rolling and grassy plains of Scythia did they fly, above the rivers Thermodon and Hyspanis. Erelong, the level prairies gave way to sandy deserts of the color of cinnamon, and a wall of Smoking Mountains could be discerned at the eastern horizon. Judging them to be sufficiently beyond the reach of the Efreet at this point, and becoming weary, they then by mutual decision, reached by gesturings, descended, for the hospitable and welcome greenery of an oasis had appeared beneath them amid the dusty tracts of desertland which stretched to either side.

Landing once again on solid earth (which the Paynim, flinging himself precipitously from the saddle, made haste to embrace and to cover with blubbery kisses, being most unused to flying), they dismounted and led their beasts into the gardenlike plot.

"Oh, how lovely!" exclaimed the Princess Arimaspia, clasping her white hands together in the scented valley between her white breasts. And in sooth the oasis presented a most appealing aspect to the exhausted and saddle-weary travelers. A lucent pool of pure water lay enframed in glossy greensward; flowering fruit trees bent above the water as if to admire their fruitage in the glassy mirror, and tall palms nodded in the evening breeze. The heavens above darkened to the purples of evening, and a Shooting Star traced its brief but brilliant track of silvery fire adown the dusky skies. Peace, obviously, and rest, reigned in this bower.

They unburdened their steeds, and the Hippogriff, at least, was led into the shallows to disport and to refresh itself, while the others relaxed upon the dewy sward and caught their breaths.

So pleased to be safely away from the enchanted palace of the blue Efreet was he, that Pteron quoted lengthy aphorisms and apothegms from the works of those noted authorities, Calphurnius Bassus and the famous historian, Alcofribas Nasier.

So relaxed and amiable did Kesrick feel, that he did not even become wearied.

XII
THE TREACHERY OF GAGLIOFFO

After the luncheon which they enjoyed earlier, and which had been unexpectedly doubled, due to the surprise discovery of the Scythian Princess and the disenchantment of the Paynim, the supplies of nutriment which the sorcerer had prudently packed away in the wicker baskets slung across the hindquarters of the Magic Horse were more than considerably depleted.

Therefore, while the Princess Arimaspia and Sir Kesrick diligently searched among the blooming trees of the oasis, hoping to find additional provender to swell their feast, Gaglioffo and Pteron unpacked what little viands remained undevoured. There yet remained a bottle or two of the red wine of Schiraz and the white wine of Kismische yet unbroached, and certain jellies and comfits and sweetmeats. These were laid out on a spread cloth, and when the young lovers returned, bearing melons, citrons, mangoes, coconuts, and a variety of nuts and berries, the table was complete.

And thus it was that they dined, while above them twilight erected its dome of shadows and silences, and the first wan and trembling stars ventured forth, and the full moon rose like a globe of luminous silver, to caress the sands of the circumambient desert with its pure and frosty rays.

"Tell me, Princess," requested the sorcerer Pteron, leaning comfortably on one elbow and sampling the sweetmeats with his other hand, "as you are presumably knowledgeable in these regions of the world, what desert is this, if you know, and in what nation?"

Arimaspia prettily contorted her ivory brows in a little frown. "Sir Sorcerer," she spoke up thoughtfully, "it may well be one of the sandy wastes which adorn the bosom of the most northerly parts of the famous Kingdom of Persia, or, perchance, of the most southerly portions of mine own native

Scythia. One desert looks, after all, very much like any other desert, and as the cold wind made mine eyes water, during our flight hither, I did not really have a chance to peruse the landscape."

Pteron nodded, having arrived at very much the same conclusion, himself. "When we have completed our repast, then," he said amiably, "and have rested a bit from our perils and exertions, it is my intention to return to my house in Taprobane, while Sir Kesrick, I doubt me not, intends to direct his Hippogriff on the long flight into the West, where his ancestral home reposes among the valleys and fields of the country of the Franks."

Kesrick blinked sternly at this unexpected remark.

"Magister, we can hardly abandon the Princess of Scythia to whatever horrible fate may await her here in these lion-guarded wastes, and neither will the laws of chivalry permit us to desert poor Gaglioffo in similar straits!" he protested.

"Come, come, my dear sir," puffed the sorcerer; but the knight of Dragonrouge would not be overruled.

"The laws of chivalry are clear and exact upon precisely this problem," he asserted. "Having rescued a Princess from a monster, one is obligated, by the knightly code, to see her safely home to the bosom of her family, and very much the same obligation exists between a wizard who has been fortunate enough to disenchant a poor and hapless fellow like Gaglioffo, here, whom we must certainly escort to a place of safety."

"The agreement between yourself and me, Sir Kesrick, only covered that period of time in which our interests were mutual," said Pteron. "Which is to say, the quest and discovery of the talismans which interest us; that quest having fortunately terminated in success, we are, both of us, free to go our own ways. If you feel honor-bound to escort the Princess to the Scythian capital, or this fellow to some civilized country, that is entirely your own decision, and does not effect myself."

Kesrick bent upon the sorcerer a severe disapproving gaze.

"Upon the obligations of gentlemen," he said in stern and unrelenting tones, "I can only cite the eloquent and eminently reasonable arguments of Zorobasius, which are, as you will recall, irrefutable."

"But—!"

"And, moreover, in these same arguments, the distinguished Ptolemopiters assents, in a treatise (which, if you have not had the opportunity to peruse, I must recommend to one of your discernment) wherein he amply demonstrates the purest reason and logic behind the earlier discourse—"

"Oh, very well, very well!" said the sorcerer hastily, and that was an end to the matter.

On most subjects the amiable youth could be persuaded this way or that, the sorcerer had already discovered, but when the question at hand hinged on anything relating to the laws of chivalry, he became adamantine.

"I have not yet had the opportunity to scrutinize closely your magic jewel," said Pteron. "May I have a look at it?"

Kesrick removed the pommel-stone from his wallet, where he had put it away for safekeeping, and handed it to the sorcerer, who peered at it through a small but powerful lens.

"Excellent worksmanship, indeed," he murmured after a time, "and it now occurs to me that I have heard of such a talisman before."

"Indeed?" said the young knight in polite inquiry. The sorcerer nodded in a positive manner.

"Yes, yes," he puffed excitedly, "I am quite certain; in fact, I would stake my thaumaturgical reputation on this matter. Young sir, what you have here is one of the most powerful and celebrated of all the famous talismans of antiquity: for it is none other than the Pantharb itself, the former prized possession of the Hindoo magician, Iarchas, who owned it back in the days of the noted Appolonius Tyanaeus. Among its other powers, it has the unique property of reflecting any malign enchantment back upon the enchanter who cast the spell in the first place. I at last understand exactly why the villainous Zazamanc wished to deprive you of its protection, for otherwise he would not have been able to work any magic against your person, at dire peril of his own safety."

"Well, well," smiled Kesrick, impressed. The sorcerer handed the fiery-colored jewel back to its owner, who again placed it in his leathern wallet. Neither of them, being engrossed in studying the pommel-stone, had noticed the wily Gaglioffo edging near as if eavesdropping on their conversation.

By this time night had fallen and they all felt much too weary from the many venturings and exploits and perils of the long day to continue on their journey to the famous capital of Scythia and decided to spend the night in this pleasant spot. From his wicker baskets, the sorcerer produced warm blankets and each of the adventurers rolled up in one of these and promptly fell asleep.

All, that is, save for one of them.

The sun had already lifted above the edges of the world when they awoke from their deep and refreshing slumbers the next morning, and it was not long before the sorcerer and the knight made a number of depressing and disastrous discoveries.

"Where in the name of Deggial is the Magic Horse?" demanded Pteron in astonishment, for the ebony creature no longer stood near the graceful palm tree to which he had yestereve tethered it.

"For that matter, Magister," Kesrick exclaimed in fearful shock, "where is the Princess Arimaspia?" For she, too, was not to be seen. But there were her empty blankets, beneath the fragrant jessamine bush where she had lain.

A dreadful surmise struck both of our heroes in the same instant, and they turned to observe that Gaglioffo, as well, was missing.

"By Ampharool!" cursed the sorcerer in tones of extreme bitterness, "but the rascally black-avised scoundrel has made off with your Princess and my Magic Horse! Doubtless the villain has flown to Scythia, to claim the reward offered for rescuing the Princess Arimaspia from the Rosmarin, as well as to demand her hand in marriage—did you notice how the scoundrel eyed the young woman in poorly concealed lust, whenever he could do so without believing himself observed by either of us?"

"I did, indeed, but thought little of the matter," groaned Sir Kesrick, who was charitably inclined on this point, since he could hardly imagine any man who would not have stared at the beautiful sixteen-year-old Princess of Scythia, especially since she still scorned any proffer of raiment and went about attired in nothing but her own loveliness.

Digging in his wallet, he made another horrible discovery.

"The magic pommel-stone of famous Dastagerd is missing, too," cried the youth in tones of complete and utter despair.

Pteron searched the pockets of his robe in grim silence, and, of course, discovered that the Ring of Soliman Djinn-ben-Djinn was also to be listed among the objects purloined during the night by the wicked Paynim.

"The absolute scoundrel!" muttered the sorcerer. "Well, he

was aptly named, and I should have suspected the truth of him all along."

"Whatever are we to do now?" asked Kesrick, crushed to the depths of despair by these dismal and depressing discoveries.

"Your Hippogriff can bear us both upon his back, for he did not seem greatly to tire beneath the added burthen of the Scythian Princess, and I am no heavier," observed Pteron.

"In that case, I suggest we depart at once for the Scythian court to expose this vile impostor," cried Kesrick. Such was his eagerness to rescue the beauteous Arimaspia from the clutches of the rascally Paynim, that he did not even pause to break his fast.

In less time than it takes to tell the tale, they were awing and away, soaring across the burning sands in the direction of the capital of Scythia.

While these events had been taking place, you need not for one moment suppose that Zazamanc the Egyptian wizard had been idle or had relaxed at all in his various villainies. Indeed, the very moment that the magic cloud conjured up by Pirouetta the Fairy of the Fountain had plucked the Frankish knight from his grasp, and without even pausing to vent his frustrations by laying waste to the countryside or leveling Dragonrouge itself, the wizard instantly repaired in his iron chariot, drawn by a matched team of Wyverns, to his subterranean palace beneath the burning sands of the Moghrab, and began consulting the oracles of sortilege in order to discover the whereabouts of the Frankish knight.

He had at length found Kesrick in his magic crystal, a black mirror of polished obsidian which reposed in a frame of iron worked all over with the grinning visages of demons. By means of this crystal he had followed the adventures of our hero, even as I have related them, and now crouched atop a tall stool whose legs were made from the thigh-bones of his vanquished enemies, pondering a vast tome which lay open before him upon a narrow lectern fashioned from the rotten wood of gallows and coffins. Above his head there dangled by a length of iron chain a retort of glass filled with clarified phosphorus, whose coldly weird effulgence fell upon the great book he was feverishly perusing, as it likewise shed its uncanny luminance on dripping walls of ragged stone, where skeletons dangled in rust-eaten chains.

"This Pteron is a clever fellow, by the Fiend Asmodeus!"

swore Zazamanc in his harsh, grating voice, tugging viciously at the end of his long stiff beard, "and now that the vapid young chevalier has managed to recover his accursed pommel-stone, I dare not intervene in his adventures. . . ."

A gleam of cunning came into his black, wicked eyes, and he lay one gnarled finger along his jutting beak of a nose.

"But if I dare not intervene in person," he said slyly to himself, "perhaps I can enlist the aid of an accomplice to perform as my surrogate!"

Springing from the tall stool, he strode across the dungeon floor and tugged at a length of hangman's rope. From the depths of the subterranean palace a bell tolled mournfully, and erelong there came in answer to this summons the dragging footsteps of a cadaver animated by Black Necromancy, whose rotting visage was pullulating with maggots.

"Prepare the iron chariot for my immediate departure," the wizard commanded.

XIII

WED AND WIDOWED

Even as Kesrick and Pteron had assumed, it was none other than the villainous Gaglioffo who had carried off the two magic talismans and the Magic Horse, which he was able to operate, having closely observed the sorcerer manipulating the various knobs and pegs that directed the ensorcelled steed. As an afterthought, the Paynim had fallen upon the sleeping Princess, and had adroitly bound and gagged the young woman before she was more than half-awake; for, as the sorcerer Pteron had observed, the rogue had conceived of a violent passion for the nubile Scythian from the very moment he had first observed her tender, and quite nude, body while in the person of the Rosmarin. His subsequent disenchantment had done nothing to alleviate his infatuation, save, perhaps, to replace one appetite with another, or so, at least, we may charitably hope.

It was not, this thievery, prompted by any particular fears of his compatriots, for the scoundrelly Paynim quite trusted the chivalrous instincts of the Frankish knight, and the gentlemanly urgings of the sorcerer Pteron—no, but if Gaglioffo was ever to express his personal philosophy, it might well have been phrased, "Mahound watches over you, but hide your own rubies." In other words, self-interest was the guiding light of Gaglioffo's miserable life, and it had rarely failed him yet.

Sometime about the mid of night, then, he had burglarized the slumbering knight and the snoring sorcerer of the two talismans which seemed so important to them, had carried off the Princess, and, now, mounted upon the Magic Horse, was traversing the midnight skies like a blazing meteor, bound in the direction of the capital of Scythia, where it was his impertinent plan to claim the hand of Arimaspia in marriage, and also to collect the very sizable fortune offered by the

King of the Scythians to whomsoever might be able to destroy the Rosmarin.

This city, called Sauromatia, was built upon the shores of the River Tanais, which the Magic Horse reached about sunrise. The river glittered and flashed in the morning sun, and the city itself was very fair, its yellow domes and minarets floating as if substanceless upon a sea of mist, perforated with tall black cypresses, and dawnlight glowed upon the marble fronts of palaces, and long arcades of shining pillars, and a veritable forest of obelisks, and lofty carven arches that spanned half-circles of the hot blue sky.

Gaglioffo landed in the palace courtyard, and immediately began making such a hullabaloo that they had to rouse the King from his slumbers. Kings are rarely accustomed to arising before noon or thereabouts, and thus, cursing and slapping the servants, King Octamasadas dragged on his second-best robe, clapped his Tuesday crown on his balding head, and ventured out onto the balcony which overlooked the courtyard, in order to discover what all the yelling was about.

Spying the crowned figure, Gaglioffo addressed him as follows:

"Monarch of famous Scythia, I am the internationally renowned sorcerer Pteron, come to claim the rewards offered for the rescue of the Princess Arimaspia, and also her hand in marriage, for I have destroyed the fiendish monster, Rosmarin, and here is the Princess herself, safe and untouched!"

With these words, he whisked the Princess from the back of the Magic Horse and adroitly removed her gag and severed her bonds with a small knife heretofore hidden in his sash.

"D-daughter, is it indeed you?" queried Octamasadas III in a trembling voice.

"Yes, wicked stepfather," spoke up Arimaspia, "but—"

"You need have no doubts as to my prevarication, O King of the Scythians," shouted the Paynim boldly, "for only a sorcerer of my fame could possibly fly about the world on a Magic Horse of ebony, such as that you see before you, or possess such important magical talismans as these"—and here he produced the Seal-Ring of Soliman Djinn-ben-Djinn and the magic pommel-stone of Dastagerd.

"Oh, my," said the King tremulously, touching his fingers to his lips.

"But he is not—" began the Princess furiously, but once again the treacherous Paynim cut her off.

" 'Twer best for you, King, that you marry us at once and hand over the fortune promised in your edict, for by the sorcerous powers at my command, I could in a twinkling transform your vaunted palace into a garbage heap, and yourself into a crow!"

"Goodness me," moaned the King, thinking to himself that some mornings it simply does not pay to get up.

"Whatever is all this clamor about?" demanded Queen Thomyris, coming out onto the balcony in her dressing-gown, with her hair all done up in curlers. Her husband informed her in terse words, whereupon the foolish and weak-willed woman cried aloud to the gods and exchanged a timid glance of endearments with her daughter, who was furiously trying to get a word in edgewise, so as to expose the rascally Paynim as the impostor that he was.

"I have little time to waste, O King, by Mahoom!" said the Paynim in ominous tones. "Before the mid of morning, I would fain return to my palace of enchantments in the Antipodes with my affianced bride, and, may I make so bold as to remind you, the fortune you offered to whatever hero might despatch the Rosmarin and rescue the Princess!"

"Oh, quite so, quite so, my dear chap!" said the King, shivering in his boots (well, his carpet-slippers, actually, as he had not taken the time to don other footwear). "Daughter, I declare you married to this valiant hero! Footman, deliver the rubies to yonder gentleman, and, by all means, permit him to depart as swiftly as ever he will to the Antipodes, whatever they are! My blessings upon you both, and pray inform us of the birth of your first-born!"

"But—" cried the Princess, a bit too late, as both of her royal parents had ducked back into the palace in order to be out of the way of any further demands by the powerful sorcerer.

Gaglioffo chuckled as scurrying and white-faced servants, delivered into his greedy hands bag on bag of flashing rubies. *This* adventure, at least, was turning out much in the manner as he had always hopelessly dreamed one of his expeditions might result: not only was he possessed of powerful magic, but also of incredible wealth, and, as well, the delectable body of the nubile and stark naked Princess was his to toy with.

It had, all things considered, not been an unprofitable morning for Gaglioffo.

However, as one or another of the philosophers has probably noted ere now, the morning was not quite over yet.

The Egyptian wizard had traversed the immeasurable leagues of the World between his African home and the aerial coign of the Efreet in a mere matter of minutes, such was the urgency of his mission. Arriving at the place in the upper empyrean, where Azraq squatted above the clouds, revolving slowly so that the vigilant gaze of his burning eyes might view all approaches to his enchanted palace atop the Rhiphaeans, he wasted no time in apprising the astounded Genie of the manner in which Kesrick and Pteron had befooled him.

"Indigo idiot! Great lump of deformity!" shrieked the Egyptian, waving his bare and skinny arms, about which live cobras were woven after the manner of bracelets, "the sorcerer Pteron has already thieved from you certain of your treasures, and is this very moment en route to the palace of King Octamasdas in Scythia, bearing with him your precious pretties!"

"By Getiafrose, say it is not so!" roared the Efreet, in a towering fury. Zazamanc assured his accomplice in the theft of the two talismans that it was indeed so, and in a screeching whirlwind, the angry Azraq instantly vanished into the east, dwindling from view with the velocity of a meteor, while the wizard grinned in nasty triumph, displaying the rotting stumps of yellowed fangs.

Whereupon, his work done for the day, Zazamanc made a more leisurely return flight to the enchanted palace, leaving it up to the vengeful Genie to deal, as he doubtless would, and in a manner involving much blood and perhaps a little boiling oil, or flaying alive with the tails of scorpions, with the malefactors.

The victorious Gaglioffo was greedily caressing the rubies with one sooty hand, while with the other he was pawing the trembling breasts of his new wife, the Princess Arimaspia, when all of a sudden things took a dire turn.

Although the sky was clear, and it was only mid-morning, the air resounded with a deafening clap of thunder, and a boiling cloud of furious black vapor rolled about, spitting forth licking scarlet flames.

And there suddenly appeared, melting into substance, the gigantic form of the indigo-colored Efreet, brandishing a scimitar huge enough to battle against either Leviathan or Behemoth (or both). He was in a seething fury, for his round eyes rolled in his sockets like billiard balls, and jets of yellow flame shot from his ears and his nostrils.

Poor King Octamasadas, who was just sitting down to an early breakfast, was suddenly shot to his feet as the Efreet bellowed wrathfully, sounding as loud as twenty mastodons. He rushed for the balcony again, muttering under his breath, "What now, what *now*—?"

Seeing the courtyard occupied by a blue Genie who stood taller than the tallest of his palace towers, and furiously brandishing a scimitar big enough to cut those towers down like saplings, the King nervously inquired what was toward.

"Deliver unto me, O King," boomed the Efreet in dire tones, "the villain Pteron! Where is this burglarious sorcerer?"

Octamasadas pointed helpfully.

"He is right there between your feet, my good fellow!" he called in quavering tones. "Please feel free to deal with him as your heart urges you—and now you must excuse me, for breakfast is served and Cook gets ever so annoyed with me when I am late for a meal!"

With those brave words, the King of Scythia ducked back into the room and sat down to breakfast in a rare good humor. "Doubtless our daughter is by now a widow," he observed to the Queen, "which means we can marry her off to the Duke of Crim-Tartary after all!"

The unhappy Gaglioffo, had been unsuccessfully trying to hide under the belly of the Magic Horse ever since the appearance of the Efreet, who now bent to pluck him kicking and squalling into the air, holding the fat rogue between thumb and forefinger.

"So you are the burglarious sorcerer, Pteron, are you?" demanded the Efreet, in a voice like the tempest. "Then come, sir, to the just punishment for your heinous crimes!"

And with that he bore away the screaming Paynim in a whirlwind of roaring fire, which dwindled in the distance and vanished from view.

In his terror, the Paynim had dropped both of the two talismans, which Arimaspia had the presence of mind to scoop up into her fists.

And it was just an instant or two later that the sorcerer

and the Frankish knight arrived on the scene, mounted upon the Hippogriff, Brigadore. Kesrick sprang from the saddle to sweep the Princess into his arms to cover her adorable face with breathless kisses.

"What has happened here?" inquired Pteron from the saddle.

"Nothing of any great import," sighed the Princess, nigh to swooning in the strong arms of her lover. "Only that I have been wed and widowed within the space of three minutes, that the treacherous Gaglioffo has met his just reward, and that I am yours, my hero," she sighed, returning the impetuous kisses of the Frank.

XIV
THE WANDERING GARDEN

The sorcerer looked about him at the empty courtyard. "Here there would seem to be a few bags of rubies some careless person has left lying about," he observed with interest.

"The reward my stepfather offered for the hero who should either rescue me from the Rosmarin, or slay the brute, or both, if possible," explained the Princess. "By rights, they should be evenly divided between Sir Kesrick and yourself."

"Well, we shall divide them up later," said the sorcerer, placing the bulging sacks into the wicker baskets. "And now, my boy, I suggest that you make your farewells to the Princess as brief as possible, since we should be gone from here before the Efreet discovers his error and returns to wreak his vengeance upon us."

"We cannot leave Arimaspia here," cried Kesrick. "We can hardly abandon her to the untender mercies of her wicked stepfather. Why, the unprincipaled rogue just married her to that rascally Paynim!"

"Indeed, I have no wish to return to the bosom of my family," the Scythian Princess confirmed. "The very next time another monster appears on the horizon, I cannot trust my stepfather not to chain me out as yet another offering. And I am more than willing to renounce whatever claims I have to the throne of Scythia; in truth," she added, with a tender glance at the young knight, "I have an intense curiosity to see what the kingdom of the Franks is like, and would enjoy seeing the famous house of Dragonrouge."

Kesrick broke into an exuberant smile at the prospect, and his arm tightened about her bare shoulders. His mailed sleeve was rather uncomfortable against her naked flesh, but Arimaspia did not seem to mind.

"Oh, I almost forgot," the Princess exclaimed. "The rogue

dropped these when the Efreet snatched him into the air." And she handed them the two talismans.

"Well, by Jarhibol and Acoran!" swore Pteron, delightedly, "You are to be commended, Highness, on managing to keep your head during emergencies." He replaced the Ring of Soliman Djinn-ben-Djinn in an inner pocket of his robe, while the knight inserted the magic Pantharb into the vacant socket on the pommel of the Sword of Undoings.

And then, without further discussion, they mounted their steeds, Kesrick taking Arimaspia before him on the saddle, and ascended into the air, leaving Sauromatia behind them.

They flew directly south, for Pteron was eager to return to his abode as soon as possible; only there, surrounded by his subservient spirits and all of his talismans and instruments of magic, might he feel safe from the wrath of Azraq. It may have puzzled his young friends why he should fear the Efreet, since he was now once again possessed of the famous Seal-Ring of Soliman Djinn-ben-Djinn, by whose power that monarch had commanded all of the three races of the Genii. The fact of the matter was that Pteron did not, as yet, know how to unleash or direct the power locked within the potent talisman, and that the mastering of the Ring would require patience, time and study.

They were now flying over the verdant plains of Persia, and, as the morning was by this time considerably advanced and as none of them had as yet eaten breakfast, they became hungry. Spying a gardenlike bower on a mountaintop, they decided to descend and refresh themselves, with which plan the sorcerer was in full agreement, believing himself well beyond the reach of the angry Efreet.

The garden was a beautiful glade filled with rose bushes and grapevines, sheltered by blossoming trees, and containing a lucent pool of clear water. All in all, it was a most peculiar thing to find upon the top of a mountain, when you pause to think about it, but nonetheless there it was.

"How lovely!" sighed Arimaspia, inhaling the odor of the roses, which were all of them in full bloom. The songs of nightingales filled the sweet air, and gorgeous Birds of Paradise fluttered from branch to branch, while splendid peacocks strutted upon the dewy sward.

Searching the garden, they found bunches of ripe grapes, as well as pomegranates, oranges, mangoes, and other viands upon which to sate their appetites, washing them down with cups of cold fresh water from the pool.

After breaking their fast, they rested on the velvet lawns shaded by flowering trees from the noonday sun, lulled into languor by gentle breezes.

"Where are we now, do you suppose? Is this not Persia?" inquired the Scythian Princess. Pteron nodded in the affirmative.

"It is indeed," said the sorcerer affably. "In fact, the splendid capital of the country lies not far off, beyond those purple hills. I caught a glimpse of it as we descended. In that city reigned and ruled those famous kings of old remembered yet in song and story: Kahmurath, the First King of the Persians, whose son Siyamak fell in battle against Demons of the White Mountain, and Hushang the Dragon-Slayer, and the all-knowing Jamschid, and the evil Zohak, who had serpents growing from his shoulders, and Feridoon and Manuchehar and—"

But by this time the two young people had fallen asleep, for a little too much dry history acts like a potent sedative on the young, and is almost as sleep-inducing as a heavy dose of arithmetic.

Pteron regarded them with an indulgent eye, for he had by now become quite fond of both the Frankish knight and the Princess of Scythia; but he was eager to return to his residence on Taprobane so as to learn the secrets of the Ring. He wondered if this might not be the most appropriate time to take his departure: after all, the quest had now been concluded to the mutual satisfaction of all, and doubtless Sir Kesrick would be eager to return to his distant home in order to reclaim his heritage from the Egyptian wizard. There was no reason why either of the young people should wish to venture to Taprobane with their mentor, since their destinies lay in the opposite direction.

Pteron was strongly tempted to depart now, leaving them to their slumbers, for he detested farewells. So, rising, he removed two of the sacks of rubies which he placed by Kesrick's feet, and paused only long enough to write a brief note of explanation, in which he asked his young friends to pardon him for not giving them a chance to make their farewells, and concluded by wishing them much luck and good fortune, to say nothing of happiness. This note he affixed to one of the sacks of rubies with a jeweled brooch from his robe. He then mounted the Magic Horse and flew up into the air and headed to the south.

Not very long after the sorcerer departed, a remarkable occurrence took place.

Without the slightest warning, the Garden detached itself from the mountaintop and floated into the heavens like a cloud of vapor. So gently did it drift into the sky that the movement awoke neither of the young people, and they dreamed on.

The Garden floated east, drifting idly upon the noontide breeze. It traveled with considerable speed, traversing the entire Kingdom of Persia, passing over the mountains of Turan, and crossing parched deserts, smoking volcanoes, snow-crested peaks, valleys, foaming rivers, fetid jungles, and every imaginable variety of terrain.

After two, or it may be three, hours of flight, the mysterious Garden settled again to earth, landing as gently as a drifting leaf.

Not long thereafter, Kesrick and Arimaspia awoke and looked about them in surprise, somewhat disconcerted to discover the absence of the sorcerer and his Magic Horse.

"Wherever do you suppose he could have gotten to?" wondered the Princess.

"I have no idea," confessed the knight, "but here are what appear to be my share of the rubies."

"And here's a note of some sort," exclaimed Arimaspia, stooping to unpin it. Strive as she might, however, she could make no sense out of it and handed it to her companion, who was equally puzzled by the message. This was because the sorcerer, rather absentmindedly, had written it in Chaldean, which neither of the young persons could read.

"I doubt me if the Efreet carried off our friend," said Kesrick, "for he would unquestionably have carried us off, as well, and would certainly not have left us either the rubies or the note. So I think we can definitely rule out *that* contingency!"

They gave the mystery up as insoluble, and decided, with some reluctance to depart, for Kesrick viewed with zest his return to Dragonrouge and the battle with the villainous Zazamanc.

"I rather hate to leave this lovely place, though," sighed the Scythian maid. "It is so peaceful and beautiful here, I wish we could stay forever."

"Perhaps we shall visit it again, say, during our honey-moon?" suggested the young knight with a tender and amorous glance. The Princess veiled her eyes behind the silken curtain of her remarkably long, lush lashes, and blushed prettily.

They untied the Hippogriff and led him to the edge of the Garden, where they stopped short, astounded at the sight which met their wondering gaze. When they had gone to sleep, they had been upon a mountaintop; now, however, they inexplicably found themselves to be in the midst of a verdant plain, and in the distance the sunlight flashed and twinkled from the jeweled spires and domes of an unfamiliar city.

Kesrick and Arimaspia exchanged a mystified look.

They became even more mystified a moment or two later, when they discovered that it was impossible to leave the Garden. When they sought to do so, they met an invisible barrier which resisted their every attempt at passage.

Kesrick felt before him, but the barrier was as impalpable to the touch as it was invisible to the sight. Although he could feel nothing to bar his way, he could not advance so much as a single step beyond the place in which he stood.

"This is *very* odd!" muttered the knight to himself. And it certainly was, for it is difficult to imagine an impassable barrier that affords no resistance to the touch: picture it, if you will, in these terms—extend your arm to the limit, with your fingers outstretched. Although no substance meets your touch, it remains impossible to reach farther; something like that was the experience which Kesrick found in striving vainly to pass the viewless barrier.

They circled the edges of the mysterious Garden, attempting at intervals to pass the barrier, only to discover themselves at length back in the place from which they had started. Obviously, the invisible wall extended entirely around the Garden, and rose to some unguessable height as well, for Arimaspia tested it by tossing pebbles into the air. These did not rebound from any unseen surface, but merely stayed their flight and dropped to earth again.

"It begins to look, my dear, as if you have gotten your wish, after all," said Kesrick dolefully, "for you expressed the wish that you and I could remain here forever, and if something unforeseen does not chance to occur, we may have to do just that!"

"Oh, dear!" murmured the Princess, a trifle wearily.

They returned to the margins of the pool and sat down again on the greensward. After all, there was really nothing else to do.

XV

A KNIGHT OF TARTARY

After a while, becoming bored of this inaction, Sir Kesrick went into the centermost portions of the Garden, where they had not as yet ventured, searching for whatever he might find there. Left alone, the Scythian Princess wandered back to the entrance and stood peering hopefully out, wishing that someone would come by to rescue them.

To her surprise and delight, she saw a knight cantering across the fields toward the Garden, and impetuously waved to him. He was tall and well-set-up, wearing a surcoat of lionskins over his glittering mail, and his features, or what she could see of them under his vizor, were swarthy but not unhandsome. He was mounted upon a fine black destrier.

He rode directly into the Garden and sprang from the saddle to salute her courteously. Amazed that he had been able to pass through the magic barrier, Arimaspia was momentarily speechless.

"Madame," he said, with a frankly appreciative look at her naked loveliness, "perceiving that you are obviously a damosel in distress, I am come to offer my knightly aid. May I give you my cloak, so that you may cover yourself with, what?"

"Oh, drat!" said Arimaspia pettishly. "Why is everyone always and forever offering me their *cloaks!* As if, with an Efreet after me, and caught as I am in this enchanted Garden, I had leisure enough to bother about fashions!"

At the mention of Efreets and enchantments, the knight's face lit up with a broad smile, disclosing brilliantly white teeth, which were dazzling in his olive-hued face. His black, slightly slanted eyes sparkled with delight.

"Ah!" he cried, "but in that case, let me proffer to you, madame, the protection of my strong arm and of my knightly sword!"

At this, she could not help but smile gratefully. "That is really very nice of you, sir," said the Princess, "but I already have one defender, a young knight of the country of the Franks. But do come in—oh, dear!" she broke off with a wail, for she realized that now the stranger knight had entered into the Garden, he, too, was as imprisoned here as were they.

It was at just that precise moment that Kesrick returned in high excitement, having made an important discovery; he was about to call his news out to the Scythian Princess, when he broke off short upon seeing the strange chevalier. The other knight, espying him, smiled and saluted him courteously, so he came up to them without drawing his sword, rather wishing he had worn his helm, since his red hair was somewhat disheveled.

"And this, doubtless, will be the noble-hearted defender of the damosel," cried the other knight. "Pray permit me to introduce myself, Sir Frank: I am hight Mandricardo, a knight of Tartary, and only son of King Agricane."

"And I, sir, am hight Kesrick, the knight of Dragonrouge, in the westernmost parts of the world," said that worthy, with a bow, "while this is my betrothed, Dame Arimaspia, the former Princess of Scythia."

"Charmed, I'm sure," said the Tartar, kissing Arimaspia's hand. "Jolly good!"

"Delighted to make your acquaintance, I'm sure," said the lady. "Although, actually, Kesrick dear, you are inaccurate; I forgot to write out a formal renunciation of my claims to the throne, since we departed from Sauromatia in such a precipitous hurry; therefore, I am still a Royal Princess of Scythia."

"Is that right?" murmured Kesrick. "Forgive me, darling." He was regarding the Tartar knight with some perplexity, and hardly paid attention to his betrothed.

"If I recall my history rightly, there was a noble paladin named Mandricardo, who was the son of King Argicane of Tarary," he said. "But he laid claim to famous Durendal, and fell in battle against the mighty Orlando; and, surely, that was a long time ago—?"

The Tartar smiled modestly. "Right-oh! An ancestor of mine, Sir Frank," he said. "We Tartars are an old-fashioned folk, and follow ancient ways: every Prince of Tartary is named Mandricardo, and, upon his succession to the throne of our kingdom, assumes the name of Agricane. My royal father is the present King Agricane XXIV, and I will assume the rule as Agricane XXV, when Fate so decrees."

Enlightened on this point, Sir Kesrick hastened to explain to Mandricardo the predicament in which they were then caught up, but the Tartar seemed delighted by the adventure, rather than alarmed.

"Enchanting!" he exclaimed. "By my halidom, Sir Frank, but this is welcome news. Things have become rather tame of late in the famous Kingdom of Tartary; all of our Giants and Dragons have died off, and one scarcely ever encounters a wicked witch or evil enchanter these days. To find myself hopelessly trapped in an enchanted garden is in the finest traditions of chivalry, and I pledge the strength of my sword arm in comradeship with yourself, and in the defense of the Princess Arimaspia."

The two knights clasped hands; and then it was that Kesrick was reminded of his discovery.

"Just before your arrival, Sir Tartar," he said excitedly, "I had been searching the middle parts of the Garden. I found the remains of a golden fence and the fallen leaves of an ivory door, and certain fragments of overgrown masonry that suggested that at one time there stood an edifice in this strange place."

"Ah, so," murmured Mandricardo with interest. "And—?"

"My most important discovery was of a cornerstone, buried under wild rose bushes," said Kesrick. "It bore a carven inscription, and as the writing was still legible (once you scraped off the lichens, anyway), I was able to read it, and suddenly all became clear."

"And what was this inscription?" inquired Arimaspia.

"It read,

THIS IS THE FAMOUS WANDERING GARDEN,
CREATED BY THE ENCHANTRESS ACRASIA,"

said Kesrick. And he looked more than a trifle rueful. "I should have recognized it," he exclaimed, "for after all, was it not by the hand of my own ancestor, the celebrated Sir Guyon, that the wicked Acrasia was foiled? This is the enchanted bower in which Acrasia entrapped and lured into her embrace such wandering paladins or knights errant as she could find, and, when weary of their love, it was her abominable practice to transform the poor wights into pine trees, or lions, or something. Once within the Garden, you will understand, the misfortunate chevaliers were barred from escaping by means of her magic, and, as our experience has told, even though this was long ago, her enchantments are still potent enough to leave us helplessly entrapped herein."

"Jolly news!" snorted Mandricardo, overwhelmed by the privilege at partaking in an adventure so chivalrous. The Scythian Princess was somewhat less pleased.

"Then is there truly no way in which we can escape this dreary place?" she asked woefully. "Must we stay here for the rest of our lives? I bethought me that the invisible barrier was dissolved when Sir Mandricardo rode in—"

The Tartar tested the barrier with hand and point of sword, and reported it to be still intact. "It would seem, Princess," he said respectfully, "that one can enter into the Wandering Garden freely, but leaving it will be quite another matter."

"Such has been our discovery," admitted Kesrick. The young couple entered into the grassy region about the pool, while Sir Mandricardo led his steed to the brink and unbridled it so that it might drink freely. Then the three sat down for a council.

"We are not likely to starve, at least," said Kesrick, and he mentioned the various fruits which they had thus far found in the Wandering Garden. "As well, toward the centermost parts, I found mulberry bushes, a mango tree, several trees bearing walnuts, and a smallish grove of bananas."

"A pity that none of us seems to be armed with a bow," commented Mandricardo, "otherwise we could bring down some of the more edible fowl I see fluttering about, and not have to do without meat. Still and all, a jolly adventure this promises to be!"

"Unless, of course, the Garden decides to remove itself to some other part of the world," observed Arimaspia gloomily. "For all we know, it might decide on the Antipodes, or Ultima Thule."

"Well, all I know of Ultima Thule, for I have never visited that island, is what I have read in the works of the noted Antonius Diogenes," remarked Mandricardo, and for the moment he reminded them of the missing sorcerer, who was always and forever citing the authority of extinct classical writers. "But, still and all, we must look on the brighter side: if we must travel in far and foreign climes, what be more comfortable manner of transport could we ask, than the Wandering Garden?"

"The Garden must possess some intelligence, however rudimentary," said Kesrick thoughtfully. "Otherwise, if it traveled about the world purely at random, it would long ago have collided with a mountain, or landed in a swamp of quicksand—"

"Or have arrived at the Boreal Pole, and frozen itself fast to an iceberg," added the Scythian Princess.

"Precisely; there must be some intelligence guiding its wanderings," said Kesrick. "If only we could direct the Garden in the regions of the world we most want to be—"

Just then they became aware of movement, and clutched at handfuls of grass; for the Wandering Garden, obviously having decided that it had by now had quite enough of Tartary, rose from the surface of the grassy plain and, at a steep angle, ascended into the middle air.

The three hastened to the edge of the magical barrier in order to ascertain the direction of the Garden's flight.

"It could take us to the Empire of Prester John, or even to the Isles of Zipangu!" shuddered the Princess.

"Or to the burning wastes of Libya," observed Kesrick gloomily, "where dwell the Anthropophagi, and the men whose heads do grow beneath their shoulders!"

"Oh, jolly good!" exclaimed Sir Mandricardo, in delight.

Traveling at a pretty good clip, the Wandering Garden of Acrasia seemed (from the direction of the sun) to be flying due west; and our adventurers looked on with mingled emotions as the miraculous bower soared above grassy plains and fertile fields, deep forests and steaming jungles, snowy mountains and sandy wastes, roaring rivers and sparkling cities, hurtling across the world.

After some considerable time, having lost all track of the countries they were passing over, the three became giddy at the landscape which sped by so rapidly beneath their keel, so to speak, and everything degenerated into a multicolored blur, so they returned to the margins of the pool to await the landing of the Garden.

"Jolly fun!" exclaimed Sir Mandricardo to himself, rubbing the palms of his hands together briskly, and obviously looking forward to Giants and the like. Sir Kesrick, a bit less enthusiastic, comforted the Princess as best he could, gloomily awaiting the next chapter of their adventures.

After a time, they became aware of a sinking sensation, and realized that the Wandering Garden was coming to rest.

But—upon what, or where, they could not venture a guess.

"Let us hope it is not in the middle of the sea," sighed the Princess, with which her Frankish lover enthusiastically agreed.

They ventured to the edges of the Garden and peered out on a tract of landscape remarkably lacking in noteworthy features. There was a grassy field of some extent, bordered by a dark wood, and beyond that the huts of farmers, or perhaps a small village, for the smoke of chimneys could be discerned on the late afternoon skies. Frankly, they could have been just about anywhere.

"Well, wherever we are, we can't get off, so I guess it doesn't matter," grumbled Kesrick, turning away from the invisible barrier.

"Oh, dear! What now?" wailed Arimaspia, clutching at her knight's arm, for a cloud of glittering white suddenly came into existence, and amidst the parting vapors appeared a remarkable woman.

BOOK FOUR

The Fairy and The Witch

XVI

THE FAIRY OF THE FOUNTAIN

The sparkling cloud appeared out of nothingness, melting, as it were, out of thin air.

Within it there stood an amazing figure, that of a thin and very old woman, attired in the garments of a bygone era. Her tiny face was painted heavily, and rouged, with beauty spots at the corners of her eyes and crimsoned lips, and atop her head, seemingly almost too heavy for her frail neck to support, there towered an immense peruke, or powdered wig, teased into fantastic shape, like a turreted castle with battlements and spires.

Her gown had a wide hooped skirt composed of layer upon layer of exquisite lace, over a wire framework, beneath which she wore innumerable petticoats. The high-heeled shoes on her small feet had diamond studded buckles of silver.

The bodice of her gown was flounced and puckered, with puffed sleeves bound to her thin arms by blue silk ribbons; jeweled orders flashed upon her bosom, and many bracelets clattered upon her narrow wrists. She was attired, in short, in the sort of gown that had been out of fashion for many generations.

In one tiny gloved hand she clasped a slender wand of sparkling silver whose tip bore a rosy and flashing star-shaped gem.

Kesrick instantly recognized her, although he had not seen her for very many years.

"Godmother Dear!" he exclaimed, starting forward as the old woman descended from her sparkling cloud with dainty, mincing steps.

"Godmother Dear, indeed!" she snorted, giving him a contemptuous, but covertly fond, glare. "Boy, I perceive that you have been getting into mischief again! In sooth, you have not greatly changed from the days when you were tying cowbells to the tail of the palace cat, and pinching the behinds of the pantry-maids! And who, pray tell, is this hussy? Why, the shameless wench is as naked as a jaybird, and, I'll warrant, no better than she should be!"

Kesrick gave the old woman an affectionate kiss on one rouged and painted cheek and turned to introduce her to his companions in misadventure.

"This is my Godmother, Dame Pirouetta, the famous Fairy of the Fountain," he said to them. They made the appropriate bows and curtsies, and Sir Mandricardo murmured, "Oh, jolly good!" under his breath.

Dame Pirouetta was surveying the Garden through an old-fashioned pair of gold-rimmed spectacles, called a lorgnette, which were attached to a slim rod of mother-of-pearl.

She sniffed. "Well, and lackaday! I perceive me that this is none other than the Wandering Garden of that lascivious hussy, Dame Acrasia! Although I always loathed her deplorable morals, which were simply depraved, I must admire her worksmanship, for it would certainly seem that her enchantments are first-rate! In fact, they are veritably perdurable."

At this, the Scythian Princess stepped forward imploringly.

"Oh, Madame Pirouetta, and cannot you rescue us from this enchantment? For we have been here long enough, and are anxious to continue our journey!"

The powerful Fairy surveyed her through the lorgnette, with a severe and disapproving glance.

"Madame," she snapped frostily, "I am not accustomed to holding conversation with young women who go about entirely devoid of clothing, even though they may or may not be Princesses of the Blood!"

"Oh, do please help us, Godmother Dear!" Kesrick chimed in and Sir Mandricardo added, "It would indeed be very kind of you, Madame!"

Glancing at Kesrick, the Fairy's stern expression softened, and she pinched his cheek and tousled his dark red locks affectionately.

"Oh, go along with you for a very fool!" said the Fairy. "Since you cannot go out by the sides of the Wandering Garden, for reason of the magical invisible barrier, did it never occur to you to go *up?*"

" 'Up'?" repeated Kesrick wonderingly.

"Certainly 'up'!" snapped Dame Pirouetta. " 'Pon my soul, I don't know what this younger generation is coming to! Observe you, pray, young man, the various fowl inhabiting this

Garden: well, and do you think they were created here? Surely, they come and go as they will!"

"Well, actually, I—" began Kesrick haltingly.

"And how do you suppose this famous sorcerer of yours got out of the Garden, heh?" she demanded in acid tones.

"He . . . he must have flown away mounted on his Magic Horse," murmured the young knight.

"Precisely! In other words, he flew *up*, you young idiot!"

"Um," said Kesrick in a small voice, looking remarkably foolish.

"Um, indeed!" said Dame Pirouetta tartly. "You will find, dear boy, on these chivalric adventures of yours, that manly courage and fortitude, even when bolstered by the fortunate possession of an enchanted sword such as Dastagerd, are not quite enough: one requires, as well, the use of logic, reason, deduction, and, in a word—*intelligence!*"

And with that parting shot, the Fairy Godmother waved her flashing wand; clouds of radiant light rolled into being, and upon these she stepped daintily, as one might mount the steps of a podium. Blowing a farewell kiss to Kesrick, she waved the wand once more, whereupon the luminous clouds gathered together, hiding her quaint figure from view, and promptly vanished into nothingness again.

"Whew!" said Kesrick, leaning against a balsam tree. The unpredictable comings and goings of his Fairy Godmother were always trying on his nerves.

"Oh, jolly good, 'pon my halidom!" said the Tartar knight feelingly.

Well, and now that our three adventurers had been given the secret of how to escape from the Wandering Garden of Acrasia, they made haste to depart therefrom, before the bower should take it into its mind to travel to the Antipodes, or to far Meropis beyond the ocean of the west. But there was one problem.

In short, Mandricardo could not take his destrier, which he was very fond of, with them, since the black could not fly and was too heavy for the Hippogriff to somehow tow into the air. The Tartar knight sorrowfully removed the bit and bridle from his steed, and the saddle and trappings as well, and bade his noble courser an affectionate adieu.

"You will be happy enough here, my Bayardetto," he said, stroking the smooth soft nose of the destrier as it nuzzled him gently. "There will be a plenty of lush sward to graze upon, dash it all, and the clear water of the pool. There's a good fellow!"

Squaring his shoulders, Mandricardo let the horse wander off to crop the greensward. No harm could come to him here, among the birds and flowers, so the Tartar cheered himself. Kesrick, on the other hand, was feeling a trifle depressed, not only that his chivalrous comrade-in-arms must bid his favorite courser farewell, but from other reasons—for it is only in the feebler fairy tales that the knightly or princely hero has to be helped out of the predicaments he gets himself in by the supernatural aid of such as his Fairy Godmother, and he privately was disgusted with himself for not thinking of exactly how the sorcerer Pteron had escaped from its toils, which was, of course, by going *up*. Still and all, there is no use in crying over spilt milk, as the poet remarks; and, besides, if they had not felt themselves imprisoned by enchantments, they would never have had the opportunity of making the acquaintance of the Tartar knight, Sir Mandricardo.

The saddle of the Hippogriff was more than a little crowded with the three of them aboard, to say nothing of the sacks of rubies which the young knight did not feel like leaving behind, but albeit on laboring pinions Brigadore ascended through the treetops and landed them a short distance outside the Wandering Garden.

"Thank goodness *that* is over!" exclaimed the Scythian Princess, with relief.

"I quite agree, my beloved," affirmed Kesrick in positive tones. He had been getting heartily sick of eating pomegranates.

"And where to now, sir and madame?" inquired Mandricardo, who was enjoying the adventure with considerable gusto, things having been very quiet in the Kingdom of Tartary of late.

Kesrick glanced about him dubiously.

"I haven't the slightest notion," he confessed, "since I haven't the slightest idea where in the world we are."

"There is chimney smoke rising from beyond that forest," observed Arimaspia, pointing. "Perhaps there is a village—with an inn, let's hope!" She surveyed her unclothed person ruefully. "I would certainly enjoy a hot bath," the Princess said dreamily, "and a night in a real bed, for a change."

There being nothing else to do, and as the Hippogriff could not carry three grown persons for very far without tiring, they proceeded in the direction she had indicated.

When they entered it, the forest seemed old, and dark, and ominously still; and the farther they ventured within the woods, the older, gloomier and more silent they became.

It seemed to the adventurers that they plodded along for an hour or more, scrambling between gnarled tree trunks, tripping over roots hidden under dry dead leaves, slipping in puddles of mud, and falling into thorn bushes.

Eventually, however, they entered a clearing and found before them a wattled hut enclosed by an iron fence with a rusted and squeaking gate. Chained by the front doorstoop was a gaunt and hungry-looking dog, who watched them narrowly but did not bark.

"Halloo, the hut!" cried the Tartar knight boldly. "Is anyone at home, what?" But no reply broke the ominous quiet which reigned in this place, and neither Kesrick nor Arimaspia very much liked the looks of things.

"Perhaps we should press on," suggested the Princess a bit nervously. "The village cannot be far."

Mandricardo pointed aloft, where sooty smoke belched from a fieldstone chimney. "Perhaps there is no village at all, Madame," he said jovially, "and all we glimpsed from beyond the wood was the smoke of this chimney. At any rate, I am thirsty, and where there is a hut, there must be a well, so, then, shall we not inquire of the peasants within as to the whereabouts of the closest town or the nearest inn?"

Kesrick and Arimaspia agreed, with some reluctance, that this appeared to be a sensible suggestion, so they opened the squeaky gate and approached the queer hut. The mangy dog slunk whining under the doorsteps as they came near, and still did not bark, which was odd behavior, for a dog. Mandricardo rapped on the front door, and, receiving no answer from within, made so bold as to push the door open, for it was unlocked. They peered in, perceiving nothing but darkness, cobwebs, and volumes of dust.

"Well, dash it all," grumbled Mandricardo, "*someone* must live here, else why is the chimney smoking?"

"Perhaps they are at work in the fields," suggested Arimaspia timidly.

"What fields?" demanded Sir Kesrick. "We are in the middle of the woods!"

"Well, since we are here, we might as well go in," suggested the Tartar knight, and in they went.

"What queer furnishings!" murmured Arimaspia half to herself. They looked around, beginning to feel distinctly out of place; for upon a shelf they observed many strangely shaped bottles and flasks, among them a large bottle filled with clear alcohol in which there floated the malformed fetus of a stillborn child, while in another, coiled as if in slumber, there reposed a milk-white serpent with three pink eyes.

On an old oak table there stood a human skull with a waxen taper atop it, but unlit; to judge by the waxen dribbles which ran down its bony rondure, many other stubs of candles had burned here. Before it lay a huge, iron-bound book, whose wrinkled parchment pages were covered with weird cabalistic signs and symbols.

"I must confess that I do not like this one little bit," muttered Mandricardo, a bit shamefacedly. "Perhaps we had better forge on, what?"

"I think perhaps you're right," affirmed Kesrick, and they turned to go. But just then the dog chained in the front yard called out, in a shockingly human voice, "Mother Gothel! Mother Gothel!" And in the next instant a barred cage, which had been suspended near the ceiling on a long chain, and which had gone unnoticed among the shadows and cobwebs, crashed down about them, and they found themselves captives once again.

XVII

THE WITCH'S HUT

Although Sir Mandricardo seized the bars of the cage and sought, with Kesrick's aid, to lift it off the floor, it was too heavy for the two knights. Whereupon Mandricardo whipped out his sword and began hewing lustily away at the bars, but to no avail, for all he accomplished was to put several knicks in his sword.

As he stood, fingering these ruefully, Kesrick motioned him aside and unlimbered Dastagerd. But the metal of the cage bars resisted even the magic blade of the Sword of Undoings, for the cage was constructed of Adamant, a metal even stronger than enchanted steel. He gave up and turned to council with his two companions.

"I am rather glad that you tied Brigadore to the fence outside," said the Tartar knight, "for it would be a bit overcrowded in here with a Hippogriff, what?"

Arimaspia was trying to think of possible solutions to their dilemma.

"Perhaps your Fairy Godmother will come to our rescue again," the Princess of Scythia whispered in hopeful tones, but Kesrick shook his head reluctantly.

"Rescuing us twice in one day would be a bit too much to expect, even from Dame Pirouetta," he observed gloomily. "And, anyway, she must have many other princes or knights among her godsons, and cannot very well be expected to always be looking after me. No, I fear we shall just have to sit here until the owner of this residence turns up."

"The dog called her 'Mother Gothel,'" muttered Mandricardo in musing tones. "I seem to recall having heard of an old crone of that name; but by all repute, she is a Wicked Witch."

"Isn't *that* splendid news," said Sir Kesrick bitterly.

They sat down and the conversation languished.

After a while, the Scythian Princess said, "I wonder in what part of the world we are, right now? We forgot to ask your Fairy Godmother that question."

"It seems to me that the Wandering Garden flew west a considerable number of leagues," said Mandricardo, "for if the bower had gone east, we would have found ourselves in Far Cathay, or even Zipangu. So . . . depending on how far it did actually fly, we could be in Crim-Tartary by now, or even in Pantouflia."

Again the conversation languished into silence as the three adventurers sat, each nourishing his or her gloomy thoughts. Eventually, they dozed off.

What roused them from their napping some time later was a most unusual and unexpected occurrence. For the witch's hut suddenly and without a word of warning, rose jerkily into the air, making all of the books and bottles thump or clatter together.

"Oh, what now?" sighed Arimaspia, clutching Kesrick's arm.

They could not see through the floor, of course, but if they had been able to do so, they would have observed an astounding sight, for the hut was now standing on two immense and scaly legs, very thin, and ending in birdlike claws. In fact, the feet of the hut bore a close resemblance to hen's feet.

Then the hut stepped carefully over the iron fence to which Brigadore was tethered, drawing from the Hippogriff a neighing squawk (or squawking neigh, just as you please) of alarm. And with deliberate steps it moved jerkily about the clearing, every motion rattling the pots and pans on the witch's stove.

The dog tied to the front steps uttered a frightened yowl. It was fortunate for him that the steps were not really attached to the hut, or he would have been dragged about by the perambulating cottage.

There didn't seem to be any rhyme or reason to the hut's meanderings: perhaps it simply felt like stretching its legs a bit.

Kesrick was searching his mind for something that his Fairy Godmother had said to him admonishingly, something about relying on your wits when strength or courage or an enchanted sword were proved of no avail in solving your problems.

"Now, what would she advise me to do in the present circumstances?" he wondered aloud to himself; and then his brow cleared and he uttered a delighted peal of laughter which made his two companions gaze at him wonderingly.

"There, there, old chap, cheer up, what?" cried Sir Mandricardo in encouraging tones, clapping the Frankish knight on the shoulder. "No reason to lose control, you know; buck up and get a grip on yourself, there's a good fella!"

"Oh, I'm not cracking up or anything," chuckled Kesrick. "In fact my mind seems to be working better than ever. I was just thinking about what Dame Pirouetta said about using your brains when brawn or blade avail you naught—and I conceived of the most perfectly splendid idea. Here, stand aside, friends, and give me as much room as possible."

They did so and he drew forth the glittering blade of his enchanted sword and began hewing at the floor of the hut. It was made of wooden planks, black with grime and rotten with age, and therefore the wood parted easily before the chopping strokes of Dastagerd. In less time than you might think, Kesrick had cut a hole in the floor large enough for them to climb through, and they saw beneath them the scruffy grass of the clearing and the scaly hen's feet attached to the bottom of the cottage, which flickered in and out of their view as the hut stalked mindlessly about.

Arimaspia clapped her hands together with joy and relief, and stood on tiptoes to kiss the cheek of her hero, while Sir Mandricardo grinned happily, clapped him on the shoulder again, and cried out, "Oh, jolly good show, what? What?"

Then they scrambled through the hole the sword had made, with Kesrick going first so that he could help Arimaspia down, and with the Tartar knight following at their heels.

The moment the dog spied them escaping through the floor of the hut, he again cried out in that weirdly human voice, "Mother Gothel! Mother Gothel!"

And this time there came an answer to his cry, in a harsh and croaking voice, like that of an ancient hag.

"Who is calling for Mother Gothel, who may it be?" screeched the voice from the darksome depths of the wood.

"It is the Dog, the Dog," cried the hungry-looking creature. "Hurry, Mother Gothel, hurry, for dinner is escaping!"

"Well, if it isn't one thing it's another," observed Sir Kesrick, hefting his sword and squaring his jaw manfully.

"Quite right, dear chap! Out of the frying pan and right into the cook-pot, what? As the fella says!" cried Mandricardo in grim agreement, drawing his own sword and lowering the vizor of his knightly helm into place.

And a moment or two later there came hobbling and limping into the clearing an old, bent woman, her scrawny bones wrapped in a hooded cloak of rusty black, leaning on a crooked stick. She eyed them craftily, while they stared at her in consternation, for she was the very picture of a wicked witch they had so often read of in their history books.

She was old and wrinkled, a very crone, with but room for the passage of a single thread between her hooked nose and pointed chin. As she looked them over shrewdly, she uttered a cackling burst of laughter, revealing toothless gums and a pointed tongue like a viper's.

"Leaving so soon, my Pretties?" shrieked Mother Gothel, hobbling nearer, "I thought surely you would want to stay for dinner—?"

At this, the Dog uttered a nasty, sniggering laugh, and, with what inward queasiness and qualms I give my reader leave to imagine for himself, the three adventurers guessed, and accurately, that they were to be the main course.

While these events were taking place far across the world, the Efreet had long since returned to his enchanted palace atop the northernmost of the Rhiphaean Mountains, and flung the weeping Paynim Gaglioffo to the floor of his great hall.

The Egyptian wizard, Zazamanc, who had been sitting on a heap of zebra skins, draped over a huge block of ambergris, impatiently awaiting the return of the gigantic Azraq, now jumped to his feet with a squawk of disappointment.

"That foul lump of quaking blubber," he hissed angrily between clenched and pointed teeth, "is not the sorcerer Pteron, you great azure-colored idiot!"

The Genie looked dumbfounded; he stared down puzzledly at the Paynim, who groveled, whining, between his monstrously huge, clawed feet.

"It's not?" the Genie uttered in deep tones like distant thunder. "But everybody *said* he was! Why, the King of the Scythians him*self*—"

"Oh, never mind, never mind," groaned the Egyptian wizard in disgusted tones. "I should have come along to make certain you didn't make a stupid mistake. If you want something done right, you had better do it yourself!" he added bitterly.

"Then," said the Efreet slowly, as his dull wits ponderously worked things out, "if this isn't the sorcerer who stole my magic treasures, who is he?"

"The humble Gaglioffo, O Master of the Earth!" cried that worthy, wrapping both arms about the Genie's big toe and covering it with slobbering kisses. "A poor and hapless Paynim who never did anyone the slightest harm, by Mahoum, and your adoring and admiring slave!"

"I suppose there is nothing else to do with this small and ugly person, but to eat him," said the Efreet broodingly, and he bent over to pick up Gaglioffo between thumb and forefinger, at which the poor rogue scampered aside and ran through the enormous arch of his legs, to fall on his fat belly before the Egyptian wizard, lustily covering his slippers with blubbering kisses.

"Save me, O Master, in the name of Mahoum, and of Golfarin, the Nephew of Mahoum!"

"Shall I eat him now?" asked Azraq dully, eyeing the Morsel and wondering how tasty a tidbit it might prove.

"No, don't bother," snapped Zazamanc, rising to his feet and kicking the Paynim in his fat ribs. "I may have a use for him later on."

And with those words, he picked up Gaglioffo by the nape of the neck and tossed him squealing into his iron chariot, which was parked nearby. Hopping in himself, and awakening his matched team of Wyverns with a blow of his long whip, he prepared to depart.

"I am returning home, you huge fool of an Efreet," announced the wizard, "and I advise you in the future to keep a closer guard over your treasures!"

And with those words the wizard turned, lashed his scaly, and hissing, and bat-winged steeds into flight, whereupon the iron chariot whirled into the air and soared out through the same wide-open window above the front door by which Pteron and Kesrick and Arimaspia had entered the day before.

Calling on Mahoum and Golfarin, and, just for luck, on Saint Adauras, the patron of those who deserved to be hanged, the miserable Gaglioffo cowered sniffling and snuffling in the corner of the chariot as the wizard flew rapidly across the earth in the direction of the trackless and inhospitable deserts of the Moghrab, beneath whose lion-colored sands, where crawled red scorpions and where slithered black vipers, he made his residence.

XVIII
CONCERNING MOTHER GOTHEL

In her enchanted house beneath the magic fountain, in the famous Forest of Brociliande, where the sorceress Vivian had long ago imprisoned the celebrated magician, Merlin, the Fairy Pirouetta sat at her dressing-table in her boudoir, rouging her chalk-white cheeks.

The boudoir of the Fairy was like an open garden, with blooming plants and small trees, bowers of blossoming roses, and its walls were insubstantial, being naught more than floating veils of gossamer and gauze. The music of violins and moaning flutes filled the air, which was rich with sweet odors of balsam and of pine, and also of the many flowers which bloomed from the velvet sward which covered the floor of her chamber, in lieu of carpeting.

As she touched up her makeup, the Fairy of the Fountain bethought her of her reckless godson, Sir Kesrick of Dragonrouge, who seemed forever to be getting into mischief, and she reached up and tapped the mirror above her dressing-table with impatient fingers.

It was a magic mirror, of course, a slim oval of silvery glass, daintily framed with worked gold which flashed with emeralds and rubies and also sapphires. At her touch, it ceased reflecting her own features, and displayed only a flow of colorless vapors.

"Show me the present whereabouts of that young rascal, Sir Kesrick," she commanded. Whereupon the Magic Mirror resolved its flux of vapors into a miniature scene, depicted in full color, and with the added dimension of depth.

By means of her enchanted looking-glass, the famous Fairy of the Fountain was able to observe Kesrick, the Princess Arimaspia, and Sir Mandricardo the Tartar knight, penned up in the cage of unbreakable Adamant in the hut of the Wicked Witch, Mother Gothel, whom the Fairy knew from of old.

"Tchah!" ejaculated Madame Pirouetta, "but it is even just as I would have expected! That feckless young idiot has gotten himself into more trouble!"

She watched interestedly for a time, as the three prisoners sought this or that means of escape from the adamantine cage, and was, of course, ready to intervene at any point, should they be placed in peril of their lives. For, while short-tempered and testy, the Fairy of the Fountain possessed a very deep affection for the young knight of Dragonrouge, and would not have sat idly by, and watched him devoured by a loathsome and haglike Wicked Witch.

She applauded silently when Kesrick used his wits and found a way out of their dilemma, helping the Scythian Princess and the gallant and affable Tartar knight to escape from the chicken-legged hut, and then she watched with close attention as the three adventurers were confronted by the cackling old crone, Mother Gothel.

The old woman came hobbling up to where they stood, studying the three of them with shrewd eyes, which were, rather disconcertingly, fiery red in color, and which lacked any pupils at all.

"Now, my Pretties," gloated the Wicked Witch, "and surely you will not be depriving a pore old woman of the pleasures of your companionship at table, for it has been long and very long indeed since pore old Mother Gothel had guests to entertain . . . and the cook-pot is full and capacious, with room enough for all. That is," she giggled, "I mean large enough for food for all of you, and pore old Mother Gothel, too, not to mention her mangy old dog!"

"Thank you, Madame," said Kesrick, "but as it happens, we have urgent matters of business to attend to on the farther side of these woods, and had best be on our way, although, of course, that will deny us the pleasures of your company and conversation, to say nothing of the tasty meal you offer, which is exceedingly kind of you."

"Pray don't mention it, I'm sure," said the Wicked Witch slyly, "for the night is nearly upon us and it will be cold and damp, mayhap, and pore old Mother Gothel would be offending the rules of hospitality if she permitted you to get away—that is, hee, hee!—to venture into the forest, which can be most unfriendly o' nights! So, young sires and tasty wench, *do* come in and warm yourselves at Mother Gothel's fire, and erelong we shall sit down to the dinner table all of us together, in one way or another, to be sure!"

"I—" said Kesrick.

"But—" said Arimaspia.

"I say—" murmured Sir Mandricardo.

"I will hear no objections, mind!" cackled the Witch, and with that she dug one gaunt and clawlike hand into the wicker basket she carried on one arm, and which was filled with squeaking Mandrakes and wriggling asps, and plucked forth a pinch of yellow powder which she brandished triumphantly before their eyes, and was about to toss the uncanny stuff in their very faces, with heaven knows what untoward results, when the unexpected occurred.

In the fine tradition of such tales as this, by the way, you will ere now have discovered from your own reading that the unexpected *usually* occurs.

It began to rain.

The very moment the first fat raindrops began splattering against the scruffy grass, the Wicked Witch paled to the color of dirty milk, and began hopping about on her one good foot, shrilling "Hi! Ha! Hee!" in a voice that sounded like long fingernails rasping upon a blackboard. They stared at her puzzledly.

Dropping the pinch of magic powder—dropping even her full basket (which overturned, permitting the captive Mandrakes to wriggle away in the scruffy grass, and all of the asps to glide to their own little hidey-holes), the Witch began hobbling and limping as fast as ever she might after her hut, which was still aimlessly hopping about the clearing on its huge chicken legs.

"Over here, you idiot! Here, curse you! Izbushka! This way, in Hecate's Name!" screeched the witch in tones of utter desperation, hobbling after the wandering hut, which paid utterly no attention to her, obviously not having been ever gifted with the sense of hearing.

"Whatever is bothering the Witch?" murmured Arimaspia curiously, clutching Kesrick's arm.

"I haven't the slightest idea, my darling," the young knight confessed, staring as bewilderedly as was the Princess of Scythia after the yelling and furiously hobbling old Witch.

The rain was coming down fairly heavily by now, and Sir Mandricardo suggested that they take refuge from the pelting precipitation beneath the lowering boughs of a funereal cypress which stood nearby. They did so, while the witch continued to hobble frantically about the clearing after her strolling hut, and the dog howled dismally from its place by the front steps.

From under the shelter of the dripping boughs, Kesrick and Arimaspia stared out into the drizzle, marveling over the peculiar behavior of Mother Gothel; for the old woman had now fallen flat upon the muddy grasses, and was thrashing about in a marvelous frenzy, beating at the wet earth with futile fists, while yowling in a voice shrill enough to shatter mirrors.

The two young people could not imagine what on earth was the matter with her, or why she should behave in such a manner, being merely caught, in what was to them only a warm summer shower. But Sir Mandricardo, fingering his chin, was frowning thoughtfully.

"I say, you two," he said, "but something has just occurred to me! Somewhere or other I recall having read, dash it, that Wicked Witches can only be destroyed by being soaked in fresh water, for some reason which escapes me, I mean to say."

"Do you suppose that *that* is what is bothering the old hag?" asked the Scythian Princess in wondering tones. Kesrick shrugged, nonplused, and they continued to observe the most strange and frantic behavior of the old crone.

Very shortly thereafter, Sir Mandricardo's supposition was borne out by the very words of Mother Gothel herself.

For she flung back her wrinkled face and stared into the pelting heavens, her wicked red eyes filled with bottomless horror and despair. "Oh! Ah! Ai!" she wailed, "I'm melting . . . *melting!*"

And indeed she was! The puckered flesh was sloughing from her face like fresh dough in a pan, and even as they watched transfixed, she began to shrink within the cover of her cloak as if dwindling rapidly in size, until soon only a small huddled shape lay under the wet cloak.

In a tiny voice, she moaned: "Oh, all of my beautiful wickedness. . . ."

Then the wet cloak slumped flat against the earth, and began to smoke and steam, and they heard no more.

As soon as the drizzle had fallen away to occasional raindrops, they left the shelter of the cypress and went over to examine what might remain of the Wicked Witch.

The Tartar knight plucked aside her cloak gingerly, employing the point of his sword. Only steaming wet cloth could he discover, for the entire substance of her bent and withered, ancient body had apparently been totally dissolved by the warm rain, even to the very bones.

" 'Pon my word!" declared Sir Mandricardo, a bit nervously. "The poor old woman, what? I mean to say, dash it all, evil as she was, of course, and not for one moment forgiving . . ."

"Look!" exclaimed the Frankish knight, pointing.

The very moment that the Wicked Witch had met her long-overdue destruction, the wandering hut sat down promptly on its folding chicken legs, or collapsed, to put it more accurately. And now it could be seen that the cottage was disintegrating in utter decay, for it would appear that the spells of the old witch vanished as soon as she ceased to exist.

The front door came off its hinges, and fell into a mud puddle. The chimney teetered awry, slumped, and came apart in a shower of old stones. The wattled roof peeled away in patches, showing a skeletal structure of old oak beams, like the ribs of a rotting cadaver.

Then the walls collapsed inward, and the hut settled into a mound of ruin.

"Oh, my!" cried Arimaspia.

Soon after this, the front steps came apart in a clatter of loose boards, and the dog got free and slunk off whimpering into the woods with his tail between his scrawny legs.

And it was all over.

"I . . . say!" gasped Sir Mandricardo. "Jolly strange, what? What?"

And his companions were forced to solemnly agree with their Tartar friend; it was indeed jolly strange, but then, they knew very little of the ways of Wicked Witches.

And closely observing these latest events through her Magic Mirror, while sitting in the boudoir of her magical house beneath the Fairy Fountain of Brociliande, Kesrick's Godmother, Dame Pirouetta, noted complacently the destruction of Mother Gothel and the safety of her godson while repairing the ravages of the day with a powder puff and rouge pot.

"Excellent work!" she sniffed to herself, with some certain

satisfaction in her tones. "That little rainstorm was just what the wretched creature required, if I do say so myself!"

And on the dressing-table near her hand, Pirouetta's magic wand flashed and flickered with rosy rays as if in mute agreement.

XIX

AT THE JOLLY FLAGON

Now that the excitement was over, Sir Mandricardo snapped his vizor up and Kesrick sheathed his enchanted blade. The magic of the spell of the Fairy Pirouetta was evidently stronger than necessary, for long after the witch had been dissolved back into her constituent elements, the downpour continued, and the boughs of the cypress really afforded less shelter than they might have wished.

Eventually, of course, the drizzle petered out and the three emerged from under the tree. While the Tartar knight poked about in the dilapidated ruins of the Witch's cottage, curious to discover what had survived, if anything, the knight of Dragonrouge tended to his Hippogriff. The creature had been sorely affrighted by the perambulating hut on chicken-legs, but became quiet under its master's soothing hands and calming words. Presently, it began sleeking back the shining bronze feathers of its wings with its golden beak, for it disliked getting wet.

Night was falling, and the west was a sea of crimson, while the first faint stars of evening blossomed like white flowers in the blue empurpling expanse above. They were all tired and hungry, but as nothing but shards of glass and bits of wood had survived the demolition of Mother Gothel's cottage (as Sir Mandricardo emerged to report sadly), there was nothing to do but to search elsewhere for sustenance and for shelter against the night.

They had seen no fruit trees or berry bushes during their trip through the woods, so obviously there was no reason to explore them more thoroughly. And by now they had come to the opinion that the smoke they had earlier seen had come, not from a town or village, but from the witch's chimney.

"Let us mount up and fly on," suggested the Princess of Scythia. "Perhaps we shall find a city or castle in which we may be invited to partake of supper, and to spend the night."

"Very well," said Kesrick doubtfully, "but poor Brigadore cannot carry the weight of three of us for very long without tiring. So let us hope that good fortune comes our way, for once, and it will be about time, too."

The Tartar knight politely offered to go about his own adventures, leaving them to continue on their quest, so as not to be an added burden to the Hippogriff with his manly weight, to say nothing of his armor, but Kesrick stoutly refused to hear a word more on the subject. He and Arimaspia had, by now, become accustomed to Mandricardo's company, and were fond of his unfailing cheerfulness and good humor.

"Very well, then, what?" said the Tartar with a flashing smile. "I will accede to your kind invitation, since you both insist. And, to tell the truth," he chuckled, "I would very much miss the end of this adventure, never knowing what had become of my friends. What a ripping good time we will have, when we finally encounter that villainous Egyptian of yours, what?"

They mounted Brigadore and flew out of the witch's wood, circling the darkening heavens and gazing in every direction, hoping to discover the lights of a city in the dusk, but failed to perceive one. Thereupon, they decided to direct the flight of Brigadore due west, for in that portion of the world they assumed that they would be most likely to encounter civilization.

After some while, Arimaspia clutched Sir Kesrick's arm, pointing ahead, and exclaimed excitedly: "Oh, look! There's a town of some size straight ahead. Thank goodness!"

And the Princess was quite correct, for as they flew nearer, they perceived a town of considerable extent, with firelight glowing through the windows of the houses and glistening on cobbled streets and tiled roofs. Not far off, a broad river ran, its clear waters sheening like silver in the luminance of the moon, which had just risen above the edges of the world.

Kesrick brought the Hippogriff to earth in the town square, hopped nimbly from the saddle, and assisted the Scythian Princess to alight from the flying steed. She looked about with interest; there was a fine bronze statue of the famous Amadis which stood in the center of the square, and chestnut trees rose from a small green park, now deserted with the coming of nightfall.

"There's an inn," she exclaimed, nodding across the square. "Do you suppose we might find lodgings therein?"

"We shall certainly ask," said Kesrick briskly. It had occurred to him that there was no real need to beg guesting for the night, not with those two fat sacks of rubies the sorcerer Pteron had left with them.

He led Brigadore by his bridle across the paved square, while Sir Mandricardo escorted the Princess. Leaving the Hippogriff in charge of a freckle-faced stableboy, who was obviously impressed with the looks of them, and was struck dumb with amazement at the fabulous winged steed, they entered the inn and found a large room with a straw-strewn floor, a low, beamed ceiling, and a warm and cheery fire roaring on the hearth.

The innkeeper, a fat man with a round red face, came bustling up, wiping his hands on a greasy apron. Kesrick doffed his helm and addressed the fellow politely, asking if three rooms were to be had, and a huge supper.

"Well, now, me lord," puffed the innkeeper, "as to supper, *that's* no problem, no problem at all! We've got us a roast steer on the turnspit, and my Meg can hustle up some baked 'taters in no time flat . . . but, when it do come to three rooms, well, we're more than a bit full up right now, as it happens—"

"Two rooms would be perfectly all right," said Kesrick, who could share one of them with the Tartar knight. At those welcome words, the troubled features of Mine Host cleared and he ducked his bald head in a pleased nod.

"Two we can provide, me lord," he said. "Pray take places near the fire and warm yerselves, while I send the scullery maid to put on fresh sheets and things!"

"Well, 'pon my word, but this is a bit of all right, eh?" said Mandricardo in jovial tones, spearing another steaming baked potato on the point of his poignard. "Decent beddin' and a hearty meal, and this wine is not bad, I've downed a flagon of worse in my time."

Kesrick, whose long legs were stretched out before the fire, so that his soggy boots might dry themselves, willingly agreed.

"Yes, and what was the name of this inn again—The Jolly Flagon, wasn't it? Aptly named," he said comfortably.

"Do help yourself to another slab of this delicious roast, dear," urged Arimaspia solicitously. "How about you, Sir Mandricardo?"

"Don't mind if I do, Madame!" said that worthy, helping

himself with gusto. Kesrick, who was mopping the last remnants of hot rich gravy from his plate with a wedge of good black bread, acknowledged that he had eaten enough.

"And, by my halidom, but isn't it good to enjoy a solid meal again," he sighed. "I had enough nuts and fruits and berries back in the Wandering Garden to last me for years!"

Just then, the innkeeper came over to inquire if they wished for anything else.

"No thank you, host," said the knight of Dragonrouge. "We are strangers in these parts, as you may have guessed for yourself, and wonder if you would be good enough to tell us precisely which parts of the world these are, anyway?"

"Why, nothin' easier, me lords, me lady," he replied. "This be the fine town of Gluckstein, and yonder river there is the famous river Gluckthal."

"I see," mused Kesrick, who had never heard of these places before. "We were flying due west, when we decided to land and seek lodgings in your town for the night, so let me ask you what lies west of here, so that we can determine our direction when we arise tomorrow."

"Well, sir," puffed the red-faced innkeeper, "on 'tother side of the river you will find yerself in a country called Orn, and a nice enough place it is, too."

"I do believe I've heard of it," mused Kesrick. "Didn't they have a rather bothersome Demon around there, some years back? I seem to recall hearing about it."

"Aye, and that they did, sir!" wheezed the innkeeper. "*And* a Ghastly Gryphon, too; but *he's* enchanted now, and perfectly safe. Can't so much as wiggle a whisker fer th' next thousand years, me word upon it."

"Oh, how ripping!" exclaimed Sir Mandricardo, his eyes shining excitedly. The Tartar knight delighted in nothing so much as hearing about knightly deeds of derring-do, unless perhaps it was having them himself. "Petrified the blighter, eh, what?"

"Summat of that kind of thing, I believe, sir," agreed the innkeeper.

Just then the little scullery maid came up to announce that their rooms were ready whenever they wished, and Mandricardo bounded to his feet, stretching his arms and yawning in jaw-cracking fashion.

"Right-ho!" he said cheerfully, giving the scullery maid a pinch, which made her giggle. "Well, I'm for bed, what say? Perhaps you two lovebirds wish to sit up before the fire and whisper endearments or whatever, but I'm for turning in right now."

Kesrick and Arimaspia were also sleepy, and rose from the table; Kesrick paid for their meal and the night's lodgings with one of the rubies from his bulging sacks; it was as big as a walnut and the eyes of Mine Host fairly popped at the sight of it.

With the scullery maid leading the way with a candle, they ascended the wooden stairs to the second story of the Jolly Flagon, said good night, and turned in.

The bed was just a little too small for both knights to sleep in the most perfect comfort, but the sheets were fresh and clean, the mattress stuffed with goose down, and there were no fleas or lice that they could ascertain. Stripping off their surcoats and removing their mail (which, like all honest knights, they polished and oiled against rust before retiring), they turned in, blew out the candle and fell fast asleep.

Except that Kesrick soon discovered that Sir Mandricardo snored.

Next morning when the three of them awoke, it was to discover a bright and sunny sky, with many small birds chirruping happily in the treetops. The two knights scrubbed themselves briskly in the washbowl the maid had left outside their door, and were attiring themselves when the Princess Arimaspia appeared, combing her long golden hair with a tortoise-shell comb the little scullery maid had shyly loaned her.

"Well, now for some breakfast, what?" said Mandricardo cheerfully.

Over a huge breakfast of scrambled eggs, rashers of crisp bacon, toasted sausages, hot biscuits with nine kinds of jam, and foaming beakers of nut-brown ale, the adventurers discussed the direction in which they should travel next.

"We were in Crim-Tartary," said Kesrick, "that's where we encountered Mother Gothel's enchanted cottage. And that means that we flew over the Zetzelstein Mountains in the Wandering Garden a bit earlier on. Beyond Orn, and farther west, lies my ancestral hall of Dragonrouge, whither I am bound."

"So west it is, then, what?" said Mandricardo zestfully. And thus it was agreed.

XX

THE WANDERING GARDEN, AGAIN

While it is true that the Marids, Efreets and Jann, the three races of the Genii, are slow of thought and rather stupid, when you have nothing in particular to do, and plenty of time to do it in, even an Efreet as dull-witted as Azraq can, in time, put two and two together, usually coming up with an answer of "four."

The huge blue fellow, gloomily pacing the halls of his enchanted palace atop the Rhiphaean Mountains of Northern Scythia, pondered the mystifying trickery that had been practiced upon him. That nice, red-headed young knight with the bright green eyes, and the blond young woman without any clothes at all, had kindly warned him against the burglarious intentions of the villainous sorcerer, Pteron. That much was certain.

After the unfortunate Deed had been done, however, and when he had flown to Scythia, to snatch from the courtyard of King Octamasadas the squalling Paynim, which everybody assured him was none other than Pteron himself, Zazamanc the Egyptian wizard had bitterly reproached him for being a gullible idiot, saying that Pteron was not Pteron.

It was quite a puzzle, for wits as unsharp as those of the Efreet Azraq.

If Pteron was not Pteron, who, then, had robbed the Garden of Jewels? For the blue Efreet had investigated, and found his direst fears borne out, for two of his most precious magical treasures were unaccountably missing.

At length, and in the fullness of time, it finally dawned upon Azraq that the one who had bamboozled him could only have been that nice redheaded young knight, who must have prevaricated, pretending that this spurious Pteron was en route to burglarize the enchanted palace, while actually the rascally deed had been performed by the young fellow, or by his nude accomplice.

"I will gnash them to morsels!" raged Azraq, when he had at last managed to figure out by whom he had been fooled. And he rose up raging, fire spitting from his mouth, eyes rolling madly in a fine frenzy.

It was not so much that Azraq really missed the two stolen treasures, for, as a matter of fact, he had long since forgotten exactly what they were; no, it was simply a matter of outrage, at having been so easily fooled.

Well, he might not know the names of the two thieves who had so cleverly purloined his treasures, but he remembered what they looked like. And, if they were anywhere to be found upon the broad face of Terra Magica, he resolved to find them, and when he did, the two miscreants would discover the full penalty exacted from those who are foolish enough to attempt to lie to the Genii.

With that vengeance in mind, Azraq wasted no further time but, drawing about himself a cloak woven of thunderbolts, he shot through the ceiling and soared into the empyrean, and began to fly hither and yon, and also to and fro, above the broad bosom of the world, searching its wide ways with keen and suspicious eyes.

While these things were happening in the Rhiphaean Mountains, somewhat to the south and west, Arimaspia, Sir Kesrick of Dragonrouge, and the Tartar knight, Mandricardo, were mounting the Hippogriff and preparing for the day's venture, having completed (to the last speck) the magnificent breakfast served to them in the inn at Gluckstein.

"Looks like a fine day for flyin'," observed Mandricardo with satisfaction, as, hands on hips, he stood in the courtyard of the inn and surveyed the azure heavens, which bore not so much as a single white cloud.

"Yes, it does that," agreed Kesrick, squinting aloft. He bent to assist the Princess of Scythia to mount the saddle, while behind him the innkeeper, the stableboy and the scullery maid waved handkerchiefs in farewell.

Well rested, Brigadore soared into the heavens, and in no time worth talking about they had flown across the small kingdom of Orn, passing over fields and farms and forests, crossed the River Eridanus, and then angled a bit more to the south, flying over Palmyria and the most southerly parts of the famous Kingdom of Persia, for Kesrick had resolved to beard the villainous Zazamanc in his den, so to speak, reckoning it wiser to have it out with the Egyptian wizard, than to spend the rest of his life wondering when, and from where, and exactly how, the wily wizard would next strike at him and his.

They flew across Phrygia, therefore, and traversed the Three Arabias and the famous land of Sheba, and over the Valley of Frankincense, and the Red Sea, and soared high above the River Nilus, and the celebrated pyramids and were about to cross the burning sands of the deserts of Libya, when they espied a familiar sight somewhat below them.

It bore the semblance of a greenish cloud of rather small size, which was floating along quite rapidly, and, oddly enough, it was flying against the currents of the wind.

"Whatever *is* that green thing below us?" shouted Sir Mandricardo above the roaring wind.

They peered over the flanks of the Hippogriff, trying to make it out, but the wind of their speed made their eyes water and everything became a blur.

"Can't see a thing, dash it all!" swore the Tartar knight, "but I *think* it was. . . ."

His voice trailed off uncertainly, and Arimaspia gave him a nudge with her bare elbow.

"Well, actually, it bore a remarkable resemblance to that Wandering Garden built by whatsername—"

"Acrasia," supplied Sir Kesrick.

"Exactly," murmured the Tartar. "Acrasia; that's the name."

They looked closely, as the green flying cloud settled gently to earth; from above, at any rate, it did seem to resemble the arbor-like bower of the enchantress.

"Oh, dear," said the Scythian Princess, "do you suppose the Garden has entrapped anyone else?"

"No way of knowing," said the knight of Dragonrouge promptly, "and, besides, we are on our way to—"

"Yes, I know," interrupted Arimaspia, "but if it has, poor creature, they will have no way of escaping from its magical toils, and may have to spend the rest of his or hers or their life in that dreary Garden, with nothing to eat except for nuts, and fruit, and berries!"

The Frankish knight sighed, but there was nothing else to do but to comply with the wishes of his betrothed, who evidently had a soft heart. Thus he guided Brigadore down into the Libyan desert and circled above the Garden, for it obviously *was* the Wandering Garden of the enchantress Acrasia, and permitted the Hippogriff to land in the midst thereof on beating, bronze-feathered wings.

They dismounted and looked about them curiously. Nothing whatsoever was changed in the enchanted bower, flamingoes and Birds-of-Paradise still flew and fluttered from branch to branch, nightingales continued to sing beautifully from the rose bushes, ripe fruit dangled from trees of mango, guava, orange and tangerine, and gorgeously colored peacocks strutted to and fro proudly upon the dewy sward. In the midst of the Garden, the pool of clear water lay tranquily mirroring the blue sky, in its setting of mossy boulders.

"Everything seems about the same as it was when we were here before," observed the Princess of Scythia, peering about.

"I suppose enchanted bowers never change very much," said the Tartar knight absently, "being enchanted, after all, what?"

At that very moment, as things would have it, the flowering bushes parted, and a tall, striking young woman stepped forth, who stopped short at the unexpected sight of strangers.

"I say!" breathed Sir Mandricardo, his eyes glowing ardently.

She was taller than any of them, save for Mandricardo, and naked to the waist, with long rippling hair and huge blue eyes which flashed with pride and spirit. In the eyes of the Tartar, at any rate, her ripe red lips looked as if they had been made with kissing in mind.

She wore high greaves of gilt bronze strapped to her lower legs and her feet were shod in supple buskins of soft leather made from the tanned hide of lynxes. A sparkling circlet of gold she wore about her brows, confining her rippling masses of long, wavy auburn hair. A girdle of linked silver plates cinched in her waist, and therefrom depended, in the manner of an abbreviated kilt, straps of leather washed in liquid silver to which iron rings had been stitched. In her left hand she bore a long javelin; a short sword was scabbarded against her thigh, and a bow of ivory and quiver of arrows was slung across her broad shoulders, the strap crossing between her bare, and rather ample, breasts.

Mandricardo privately thought her quite the most ravishing female creature he had heretofore observed, but to Kesrick's taste she was more than a trifle too Junoesque. She was, in fact, built on sumptuous proportions, and very well upholstered, especially (they noted later when she turned to lead her courser through the trees) in the hindmost parts.

She had stopped short at the sight of them, her ample bosom heaving entrancingly in consternation.

"Oh, raw-ther!" breathed Sir Mandricardo admiringly, all eyes; and, indeed, the view was a spectacular one.

"Hold, varlets!" cried the large girl in imperious tones, her javelin held at the ready. "Declare yourselves! Are you friends or foes?"

"Oh, friends, by all means, I say!" exclaimed the love-smitten Tartar. The warrior-woman looked him over with contemptuous eyes and did not lower her spear.

Kesrick cleared his throat for attention, and stepped forward doffing his helm courteously.

"I am hight Sir Kesrick of Dragonrouge, a knight of the Franks," he said with a winning smile.

"And I am hight the Princess Arimaspia of Scythia," declared that lady, stepped forth to stand at his side, with her hand upon his wrist, so that there should be no mistake as to whom he belonged.

The Amazon—for, in fact, she *was* an Amazon—turned to regard Mandricardo.

"And how are you hight?" she asked boldly.

He introduced himself, likewise doffing his helm as Kesrick had done.

"Well, then," she declared, "I am hight the Princess Callipygia, daughter of the Queen of the Amazons. And if you happen to be the dastardly magicians who enchanted this flying bower, which has borne me off against my will from my native land of Amazonia, then prepare to defend yourselves!"

"I . . . *say!*" breathed the Tartar rapturously.

BOOK FIVE

The Undoing of Zazamanc

XXI

THE SUBTERRANEAN PALACE

By this time, Zazamanc the Egyptian wizard had traversed the greater part of Terra Magica in his magical iron chariot, drawn by its matched pair of winged Wyverns, bearing the hapless Paynim, Gaglioffo, to his unknown fate.

The wizard brought his chariot to earth in a rocky and desolate gorge amid the desolate wastes of the Moghrab. Springing from the chariot, and kicking aside a shovelfull or two of crawling red scorpions the size of housecats and slithering black vipers as thick as a strong man's upper thigh, he faced a sheer cliff of rugged rock and cried in a voice like thunder, the magic phrase that unlocked the portals of his underground abode.

"OPEN, O SESAME!" he boomed. At which the cliffy wall of rough stone swung open on unseen hinges, revealing the black and yawning mouth of a cavern. Stalagmites and stalactites either hung from the lintel of this portal or rose from its doorstep, lending the black opening a remarkable resemblance to the fanged jaws of a gigantic monster.

"O, Mahoum! O Golfarin, Nephew of Mahoum!" wailed the shuddering Paynim in a paroxysm of dread and despair, cowering on the hard floor of the iron chariot. "Not to forget Dame Termagant, the Mother of Mahoum!" he added hastily.

Seizing the reins of his team, and ignoring the wailings of Gaglioffo, Zazamanc strode into the black mouth of an even blacker tunnel as the great stone door swung silently shut behind them. Torches carved from old torture-racks, and soaked in the oil of human livers and spleens, blossomed into smoky light down the length of the tunnel, and Gaglioffo, peering fearfully from between his fingers, saw that they were held by naked human arms which somehow grew out of the rock walls.

In a stall barred with iron rods, the wizard left his hissing steeds to devour their meal of worms, maggots, lice and cockchaffers, having unhitched the Wyveras. The chariot he dragged into an alcove carved from the rock. Then, dragging Gaglioffo along by the nape of his neck, he ascended a flight of black marble stairs and entered a large and capacious hall, lit by pits of flaming sulfur and brimstone.

He tossed the Paynim into a corner where a rat-gnawed skeleton hung from rusty chains, and left him to huddle weeping on a bed of filthy straw, while he ascended to his great throne-like chair, made of the skulls of babes and children mortarted together with molten lead. Seating himself therein, and tossing the wreath of living serpents wound about his arms onto one hook of an iron hatrack, he kicked off his sandals and relaxed broodingly, his swarthy brows contorted into a frown indicative of deepest thought.

Thereafter, for a time, nothing in particular happened, and Gaglioffo gradually relaxed, seeing he was not about to be roasted on a spit or carved into cutlets momently. He began gazing around him, at first timidly, then with increasing interest and curiosity.

Upon the walls of rough black rock hung mounted upon wooden plaques the stuffed heads of frightful monstrosities, much in the manner of hunting trophies.

Gaglioffo had always been a poor scholar, more interested in pinching the village girls than in conning his books, but even one so unlettered as he was able to recognize the Lamussa by his black ringleted beard and human visage and the four horns which crowned its massive brow. Likewise did he recognize by its scaled and fin-maned horselike head the Hippocamp, and the Phalmant from its blood-colored hide and hideously distorted mouth, open in an eternal and soundless howl of fury. The Strycophanes, however, and the Bleps, to say nothing of the peculiar-looking Myrmicolion, were unknown to him, even by reputation.

Behind the huge, throne-chair, where the Egyptian sat deep in thought, the crumbling coffins of Egyptian mummies were stacked like cordwood; also, there hung in iron frames wrought from coffin-nails a number of photographs of odd-looking people, all of them affectionately signed to Zazamanc, with names so distinguished that the ugly Paynim was impressed in spite of himself: the Emperor Alifanfaron, King Fayoles IV, and the dauntless Brandabarbaran, Lord of the Three Arabys. This was even more impressive than Gaglioffo could imagine, since the science of photography had not been invented yet.

After a time, exhausted from the frights and terrors of the long day, Gaglioffo curled up on the filthy straw, and fell asleep, snoring lustily.

Suddenly Zazamanc roused him from his brown, or perhaps black, study, drew on his sandals, and strode to the rear of the hall where his magic mirror hung against the wall, reflecting in somber shades the gloomy recesses of the room.

"Reveal to me the present whereabouts of Kesrick of Dragonrouge, and his companions!" he commanded harshly. The mirror shimmered with eerie blue light, swirled in a vortex of luminous colors, and resolved itself into a scene. It showed the two knights and the two Princesses in earnest discussion within the Wandering Garden. Through the interstices of the trees, Zazamanc saw and recognized the peaks of the Cassanian Mountains, and realized that our adventurous heroes had arrived in a certain part of Libya familiar to him from of old.

This did not at all displease the Egyptian wizard, who grinned an evil grin, revealing his sharpened teeth. He rubbed his bony, clawlike hands together briskly, permitting the mirror to dissolve its image into darkness again.

"Hah!" he snorted in wicked anticipation, "then they are on their way, after all! Then, when they arrive, they shall have a warm welcome awaiting them, by Tarniel!"

With that he uttered a burst of cackling mirth, and strode off into the interior of his underground castle, leaving the Paynim snoring away.

At this same time, in the Wandering Garden of Acrasia, the Amazon Princess had solicited from each of the three adventurers an account of their travels and exploits, and of the perils through which they had fortunately passed unscathed. As you already know, this took a bit of time in the telling.

When they were finished with their narratives, the Princess Arimaspia politely inquired of Callipygia her own tale of adventures. The large girl shrugged.

"Easily and quickly told, Madame," she said in her ringing tones. "I am one of the seventeen daughters of Megamastaia, the Queen of the Amazons; my country lies far to the east of these parts, in the regions beyond Hindoostan, and just before you reach the borders of Far Cathay. For uncounted ages, as you will probably know, we Amazons have denied ourselves the pleasure of the companionship of males, except and insofar as such persons are required by nature to partake in the engendering of children—"

At the thought, Sir Mandricardo broke into a rather rude guffaw, at which Callipygia broke off and transfixed him with a glare.

"We have anciently been a martial race of woman warriors, as you know," the large girl continued, "but my royal mother, unlike her famous predecessors, such as Hippolyta, Penthesilaea, Kaydessa and so on, proved to have a natural aptitude for the bearing, and very much for the nursing, of children. It is not for naught," she added off-handedly, "that the Queen is affectionately nicknamed Megamastaia of the Big Breasts."

"Rather needful, I should think," murmured Arimaspia sympathetically, "if one is to nurse no fewer than seventeen daughters!"

"Quite," said Callipygia shortly. "Well, and at any rate, when I came of age, I determined to demonstrate to the Amazonians that the ancient dynasty had not, as you might say, petered out; in brief, I resolved to be as fierce and warlike as my mother was prolific and maternal."

"Good-O!" sighed Sir Mandricardo, unable to take his eyes off her splendid attributes.

"For the last year I have ravaged the neighboring kingdoms," declared the Amazon, "battling knights, heroes and champions—so called—" she added sneeringly. "Doing battle to monsters and magicians, Giants and Ogres, and all manner of ferocious beasts. Just recently, I happened to be in the northerly parts of Tartary, in the province of Sarazin, where my misfortunate steed had the bad luck to be torn asunder by seven or eight ravenous lions, which I quickly dispatched with blade, bow and javelin."

Kesrick breathed a word or two of admiration for such a brave and prodigious feat, but the Amazon girl shrugged it aside as if it had been all in a day's work.

"Now regretfully afoot," she continued, "I wandered about the plain, eventually sighting this bowery Garden, so out of place in that bleak and barren wilderness. Approaching nearer, I espied a noble destrier through the trees; as he was uncaparisoned and appeared ownerless, I entered the Garden to investigate further. Here, let me show you—"

With these words, she turned her back on them briefly, but long enough to display those amply proportioned parts which proved that her name was as aptly given as was seemingly the case with her mother. Vanishing into the rose bushes, she emerged a moment later leading a handsome black destrier which they all instantly recognized.

"My Brayardetto!" exclaimed the Tartar knight in tones of delight. The Amazon frowned in momentary puzzlement, until Sir Kesrick added a brief explanation as addenda to Mandricardo's account of his adventures, related earlier to the Amazon in somewhat abbreviated terms. In short, they had not explained why the Tartar had been unable to take his steed with him when they had left the Wandering Garden in Crim-Tartary.

Once Mandricardo had concluded his affectionate reunion with the noble Bayardetto, Callipygia resumed the course of her narrative.

"Well, the rest of it is simply told," she said curtly. "Attempting to ride out of the Garden, I found it an impossible feat, and was forced to remain herein while the cursed thing floated hither and yon about the world, eventually coming to rest here in this desert, where you discovered me."

Since they had already explained to her why it was easy to enter the Wandering Garden but impossible to leave it unless you had wings, Callipygia at last understood why all of her strength and diligence had availed her naught in seeking to make her exit.

"Fortunately, as you can easily observe," said Kesrick, "my steed Brigadore is alate, by which means we can all readily leave the Garden at any time, although once again Sir Mandricardo will have to leave poor Bayardetto to an undeserved and doubtless an unwelcome abandonment."

"Perhaps we could rig a catapult of some sort," suggested Callipygia helpfully, being fully knowledgeable of siegecraft.

And they were still discussing the technical problems when, of a sudden, the sky darkened, thunder resounded deafeningly, and a cloud of sulfur and brimstone, through which forked tongues of fiery lightning licked hungrily, rolled down from the sky into the midst of the Garden.

XXII

AZRAQ, AGAIN

While Sir Kesrick, the Tartar knight, and the Amazon girl drew their swords and stood ready to confront whatever new and monstrous adversary had entered the Wandering Garden, the rolling murk resolved itself into a towering figure of a hideous Genie with gnashing tusks and rolling eyes ablaze like lakes of liquid lava.

"By Hercules!" exclaimed Callipygia in amazement and horror; but she did not retreat a step from the hideous creature, and neither did her short sword waver in her hand.

It was, of course, Azraq. The blue Genie had been searching the world, flying to and fro high in the heavens, his glaring eyes scanning every road and field and farm for a glimpse of the red-haired knight, the Hippogriff, or the golden-haired and thoroughly nude Princess. And at last he had found them, here in the burning wastes of the desert!

"Perfidious mortals!" he roared in tones that made the earth quake slightly underfoot, "prepare to meet your just and deserved Doom at the hands of one whom you have both robbed and deceived!"

The horrid Efreet glared down at them so menacingly that the waters of the pool trembled, violently agitated, and the very rocks about the pond contracted in terror, shuddering with a noticeable palpitation, oozing all over with the clammy perspiration of fear, while the blossoms on the flowering bushes closed tightly.

The monster grinned evilly, flexing huge hands whose nails, adept at ransacking cemeteries, resembled enormous sickles. Their lives, they knew, were to be measured in moments; but the four adventurers stood their ground, preparing to fight the fiend as best they could.

With those words, he spread his clawed feet wide, pushing over several palms and a pomegranate tree, and took his stand, lifting a scimitar of flashing steel, longer than an oak is tall, above his head. In another instant, that terrible blade would fall like a thunderbolt upon them, and their adventures would be finished, at least in this world.

But a flying shape swooped from heaven to intervene, its lineaments blurred by the speed of its descent, and a slim wand effortlessly struck the huge blade aside, and sent it spinning away into the hills.

"Magister!" cried Kesrick with delight and relief.

For it was indeed the slender, robed sorcerer Pteron, mounted upon his magical ebony steed. He gave a friendly salute to the young knight and the Scythian Princess, glanced curiously at Mandricardo and Callipygia, and descended to earth in a graceful spiral while the Genie stood as if struck to stone, eyes goggling down at him incredulously.

Dismounting from the Magic Horse, Pteron wasted no time in speaking to his friends, but turned to confront the giant blue form.

"I adjure and command you, Unclean Spirit," he shouted in stern and ringing tones, "to forever abstain from doing any harm or mischief to these mortals or their descendants, if any! By this token do I thus require your instant obedience—"

And he shrugged back the sleeve of his robe to display the huge gold Seal-Ring of Soliman Djinn-ben-Djinn, which he wore about his upper arm, just beneath his shoulder, like an armlet.

With a howl of mingled fury and fright, Azraq recoiled, instantly recognizing the talisman and realizing, from the subtle phrasing of Pteron's words, that the mighty sorcerer had unlocked the secrets of using the Ring.

"I swear to obey your words, by Kashkash and Getiaphrose," rumbled the Genie, making an humble obeisance.

"Then begone, and bother us no more!" commanded Pteron. Fiery clouds of stenchful sulfur-smoke boiled about the huge legs of the Efreet, and rolled into the sky, disappearing from sight.

"I . . . say!" breathed Mandricardo a bit shakily, putting his sword away.

"Eloquently put," nodded Callipygia, a trifle subdued.

Pteron turned to greet Kesrick and Arimaspia, who were delighted to see him again, especially under the circumstances, and they introduced him to Mandricardo and the Amazon girl.

"Charmed to make your acquaintance," the sorcerer murmured politely, shaking hands with the grinning Tartar. Kissing Callipygia's hand, he said, "*Enchanté*, madame!" She blushed rosily, unaccustomed to such courtesies.

Arimaspia was so pleased to see the old sorcerer again that she impulsively threw her arms around his neck and kissed him on the cheek. "We had no idea what had happened to you, or why you left us so precipitously!" she cried. He blinked at her.

"Why, didn't you find the note I left?" he asked puzzledly. "In it, I explained that it would take me a few days of study in my library to master the mysteries of the Ring and be able to use it properly, and that I would look you two up when I had thoroughly mastered its secrets."

"The note," said Kesrick briefly, "was written in something that looked a lot like Chaldean."

"Oh," said the sorcerer. Wishing to change the subject, he glanced around him curiously.

"Odd! This looks very much like the oasis I left you in, but that was on a mountaintop in Persia . . ."

Kesrick explained briefly about the Wandering Garden of the enchantress Acrasia, and, of course, while Pteron had never seen it before, he knew all about it.

"Well, I must get back to work; but I shall keep an eye on you, from time to time," he promised, mounting the Magic Horse.

Mandricardo cleared his throat and whispered something to the Frankish knight. Kesrick nodded, and entreated the sorcerer to assist them in somehow getting the Tartar's destrier out of the Garden.

"Nothing easier," smiled Pteron. "Unlike your Hippogriff, the Magic Horse is tireless and possessed of prodigious strength." In very little time, they rigged a strong net out of woven vines into the middle of which Mandricardo led Bayardetto. Looping the corners of the net over the saddlebow of the Magic Horse, Pteron guided his steed into the air and deposited the destrier on the burning sands outside the Wandering Garden. Then, taking Mandricardo and Callipygia on his ebony steed, Pteron flew them out of the Garden, while Kesrick and Arimaspia followed astride Brigadore.

No sooner had this been done, than the Garden floated

away in the general direction of the country of the Cimmerians.

Not very long after that, Pteron made his farewells, and then his departure, and dwindled into the distance, bound for Taprobane and home.

Our heroes, and, of course, heroines, mounted up and rode in the direction of the Moghrab. Kesrick bore Arimaspia before him on the saddle-bow, and spent much time murmuring sweet nothings in her blushing ear, except, of course, that to her what he had to say seemed very important, indeed. Mandricardo gallantly offered the same position to Callipygia, but the Amazon girl curtly refused, and mounted up behind him. The Tartar was rather sorry to have to miss the delectable sight of all those ample curves jiggling and swaying to the pacings of his steed, but there was nothing else to do but comply with what grace he could muster.

I shall not bore my reader with a lengthy and drawn-out description of the lands and peoples they observed in their travels. They crossed the River Cinyps and went through the country of the Macae, who were shaggy and bearded and went about clad in bristling goat-skins; they passed through the lands of Adyrmachidae, who bear sickle-shapen swords and who carry many-colored shields; they traversed the region of the Gaetulians, who can tame the fiercest of wild lions with mere words; and they crossed the kingdom of the Marmaridae, who are men possessed of strong magic, armed with spells that can unvenom serpents.

They made a hurried trip through the country of the Anthropophagi, not even pausing to have lunch, for fear that they themselves might become the main course; they rode through the lands of the Cynocephali, who are hairy little men who inhabit trees and have the heads of dogs; they galloped through the country of the Pygmies, where men grow no taller than your knees; and they cantered through the nation of the Blemmyes, a people who possess broad shoulders but they have no heads at all, and only the faintest suggestion of facelike markings traced upon their broad chests.

It was beyond the country of the Blemmyes that they encountered a rare Sadhuzag, a huge black staglike creature with seventy-four slim white horns sprouting between its ears, and these horns are as hollow as flutes. Fortunately, the Sadhuzag stood facing into the south wind, and therefore the music of the wind blowing through his crown of white horns produced soft and dulcet tones, which so charmed the hearer that venomous serpents were entwined lovingly about his legs and a colony of bees had taken refuge in his beard, seeking the source of such sweet sounds.

Had the Sadhuzag been facing into the north wind, of course, the sound of the breeze rushing through his hollow horns would have produced such a horrible and roaring dissonance that, upon hearing the noise, rivers have been known to remount to their sources.

It was in the very next country that they encountered a Pastinaca, a huge and furry beast like a monstrous weasel, larger than an elephant. Sir Mandricardo and the Amazon girl, who were leading the way at the time, sprang from the saddle of Bayardetto to do battle with the beast, for Callipygia was bored and restless, it having been quite some time since she had last fought a monster. As for the Tartar, he was eager and anxious to display his martial prowess before a woman whom he so very much admired, but who seemed to disdain mere men as an inferior branch of the human species.

Fortunately, the Pastinaca was downwind of them, otherwise the encounter would have had a different and more tragic ending. The Pastinaca, as you probably know, emits such a horrendous stench that the stink of its body can blight and wither trees half a mile away.

When the weasel monster made a pass at them, Callipygia, who was really more than a bit out of practice, tripped over a rock and fell flat on her stomach, which not only knocked the wind out of her but also made her drop her sword. Delighted, Mandricardo sprang to her defense; bestraddling her recumbent form, he wielded his blade so lustily that the Pastinaca, bleeding from a score of wounds, retreated in all haste, and the wind did not shift directions until it had vanished from view in the haze of the horizon.

Mandricardo gallantly assisted the Amazon to her feet again and retrieved her sword for her; as for Callipygia, her voluminous bosom was heaving with a commingled mortification, embarrassment, confusion, and the like. The tumult of her emotions was such that it caused her to mutter her thank-yous with downcast eyes, biting her lips and blushing crimsonly.

"Tut, don't mention it, all in a day's work!" said the Tartar knight, saluting her cheerfully. Then he gave her a leg up, remounted himself, and they rode on.

Thereafter, they entered into a hostile wilderness where nothing grew but thorns and poison ivy, and where nothing lived but loathsome vermin, wriggling vipers, and enormous scorpions. Human skulls and bones were littered so thickly about the dry sands that they were as common as bits of gravel in the bottom of a fishpond.

By these signs and tokens, they knew that they had entered into the trackless deserts of the Moghrab, and were probably not very far from the underground dominions of the Egyptian wizard, Zazamanc.

Nor were they incorrect in this assumption.

XXIII

GAGLIOFFO REPENTS

While these events had been taking place on the surface, in the subterranean palace of the Egyptian wizard, they went not unobserved. Hour after hour, the wizard Zazamanc stood watching the progress of our adventurers through his Magic Mirror, muttering to himself in Hieroglyphic.

Gaglioffo, in the meanwhile, had become his valet, his butler, and his slave. It had become his task to groom the Wyverns which drove the wizard's iron chariot, to oil and feed the serpents which customarily wreathed the wizard's brows, and to order about the shambling animated cadavers who had heretofore served as Zazamanc's domestic staff.

All of these tasks Gaglioffo perforce performed, but shudderingly, and squeamishly, while watching and waiting hopefully for a chance to escape from the clutches of his cruel master. Escape, in all honesty, seemed impossible: only Zazamanc knew how to open the stone door, to which more than once the Paynim had whispered the magic phrase without result. And even should he be so fortunate as to discover an egress from the underground castle, it would be to find himself marooned amid the grisly and hostile deserts of the Moghrab, many leagues from the nearest town or city. But he watched and waited; for it had occurred to the wily Paynim that he might, in time, discover the secrets of his master's power, and rob him of those rings or talismans by which he commanded the cadavers and the forces of nature themselves, thus disarming the vengeance of Zazamanc.

The underground palace contained many suites and rooms and antechambers and winding corridors and dungeons. Exploring the extent of the subterranean abode, Gaglioffo found rooms filled with huge moldering tomes, or chemical apparatus beyond his understanding, or museums of queer fossils, minerals and oddities.

There was a chamber walled with many mirrors, each of which gazed forth on the weird landscapes of other worlds or distant ages. And chambers filled with articulated skeletons, unbodied but living brains preserved in vats of nutrient froth or the stuffed bodies of uncanny monsters such as the Paynim had never before seen or heard of, or rooms called Conjuratoriums, where pentacles and cabalistic signs and circles were inscribed on the floor, and it was in these rooms that the Egyptian wizard summoned into his presence angels or demons, genii or elemental spirits, or whatever.

Certain rooms were locked with locks that had no keyhole, only the bronze facsimile of a human ear; and Gaglioffo correctly guessed that these locks were only opened by whispered Words of Power, not by material keys. What lay behind these sealed portals was unknown to him, and the doors themselves were impregnable.

His own abode, incidentally, was a miserable kennel in the rear of the kitchen, which he must share with Zazamanc's pet Werewolf, a mangy and ill-kempt creature with mean eyes and a vicious snarl, who turned into a human being once every day, and with whom the miserable rogue occasionally had conversation. He learned nothing of interest or import from his grisly kennelmate, for the creature, in its bestial form, was not capable of articulate speech, and even in its man-shape, remarkably ignorant and surly, not given to conversations of any length.

Besides which, his (or its) eating habits were disgusting.

There was another room of immense extent, a domed cavern, actually, filled with barred cages and stalls: herein, the Egyptian wizard kept his personal menagerie of rare and curious beasts, birds and reptiles. The collection included a monstrous, milk-white, pink-eyed bewhiskered serpent called a Piast, which lay drowsily coiled in its own huge tank; a soundproof iron-walled cell held another curious creature called the Phalmant, which howls so loudly that, in the extremes of its bellowings, it can burst its own belly; a smaller terrarium, whose interior you could only observe through angled mirrors, contained a small and harmless-looking and rather attractive lizard, of the hue of violets, with a three-lobed crest, like a cock's-comb. This was a deadly Basilisk, whose unimpeded gaze can strike the viewer to marble in instants.

All of these curiosities, and many more which Gaglioffo had never seen or heard described before, were used by the wizard in his experiments, that is, he employed their droppings or their saliva, or their urine, or whatever else excreta, as ingredients in his potions, elixers, and concoctions. And all of these became Gaglioffo's responsibility to feed, water, and clean up after.

The bow-legged little Paynim found his slavery in the subterranean palace all but unendurable, and dragged himself, groaning and whining and complaining to heaven (or at least to Mahoum, Golfarin, Termagant, and his other Paynim idols).

The underground castle itself was a grisly place, where rotting corpses dragged themselves through dripping, slimy halls and corridors upon unguessable errands, and where filth and fetid matter were piled about in puddles, heaps, mounds and moldy stacks.

In no time worthy of relating, he found himself with a head-cold, however, which helped to render, however temporarily, his nostrils insensible to the stenches and foulnesses amid which he toiled and labored in the wizard's service.

Actually, he saw little of his villainous master, who was busied with dire preparations for the expected arrival of Sir Kesrick and his comrades-in-arms. What these preparations might be, Gaglioffo had no inkling, but that they were deadly and dangerous he assumed from the smirks and grins and bursts of cackling laughter his Egyptian master emitted as he buried himself in books of spells and recipes, in conjurations, suffumigations, rites and rituals and ceremonies better left undescribed, as my readers may be reasonably expected to possess stomachs no less squeamish than our unhappy Paynim.

Now was the wretched Gaglioffo, in truth, paying a high price for his villainies and treacheries, and no one realized it more than did he. For, dastard and coward to the core though he indeed was, Gaglioffo was not without intelligence and was even capable, in certain extremities, of some degree of honest insight into his own character and its numerous flaws. His life had been a hard one, and in its span he had erenow stooped to deeds of theft and betrayal and cozening we shall not go into.

Often, while slopping the Gryphons or mopping up after the Cockatrices, was he wont to woefully ruminate on how well and generously he had been treated by the bold young

Frankish knight, the tender-hearted Scythian Princess, and even by the not-unsympathetic sorcerer Pteron. They alone in all the world had taken pity upon him, when hopelessly imprisoned by enchantment in his Rosmarin-form. They alone had freed him from the spells of Abaris the Hyperborean. And they had even permitted him to join with them in their quests and adventures.

And how had he repayed them for these kindnesses and considerations? By betraying and robbing them!

In the misery of his abject slavery to the Egyptian wizard (who was, all things considered, a particularly hard and unfeeling master to serve, demanding, as he did, the highest caliber of service in return for the meanest and most miserable recompense), Gaglioffo often had good reason to upbrade himself for the thankless way in which he had repayed the kindnesses of Kesrick and his friends; bitterly now did he regret his actions. But now, of course, as was usually the case with late-reformers such as the unlucky little Paynim, it was much too late to repent or to undo the mischief he had caused.

Still and all, he watched and waited and bided his time. Sooner or later, the crafty rogue whispered slyly to himself, he would discover the secrets of Zazamanc's power, and might disarm the Egyptian wizard of his potent sorceries, and make his escape to happier climes, where more careless merchants went about with fatter purses than any yet known to his broad experience.

You will observe, I think, that repentance is seldom whole-hearted, and generally arises from such base and ignoble motives as feeling sorry for yourself in dire circumstances.

Still and all, let us give Gaglioffo the benefit of the doubt, for the story has not yet reached its end.

While these events were taking place within the small and mean and miserable heart of Gaglioffo, our friends were making their way across the drear and hostile wastes of the Moghrab.

No further adventures, or strange peoples, or terrific monsters arose to oppose their passage through this wilderness. It was seemingly too barren and desolate to afford any but the loathsomest forms of crawling or scuttling or slithering life. Mandricardo, for one, resented this, for he would dearly have wished for the opportunity to again distinguish himself in the eyes of the beauteous Amazonian Princess, as he had done earlier when he had so manfully done battle against, and driven into precipitous flight, the enormous and stinking Pastinaca.

Alas for his romantic hopes, no further opportunity for heroism presented itself through the leagues of desolation wherethrough they journeyed to reach the abode of the arch-villain, Zazamanc.

Now were they entering into a region of gaunt cliffs and fang-sharp peaks, which clawed at the leaden sky. Not even the lowliest of molds or lichen or cacti flourished here, among the tumbled slabs and boulders, the sheer stone walls of the cliffs, or among the needle-sharp peaks. And Kesrick had a premonition that they had almost reached their goal; for had *he* been an evil magician (he reasoned to himself), he would have selected just such a drear and desolate region to make his habitation, and the site of his black necromancies.

Before the world was more than an hour older, his guess was proven right, as things turned out. For they turned a corner to find themselves in a blind pocket, facing a sheer wall of dark stone. And our adventurers perceived an ominous inscription carved into the cliff wall before them.

It read:

KNOW, O RASH AND FOOLISH TRAVELER, THAT THIS IS NONE OTHER THAN THE FAMOUS SUBTERRANEAN PALACE OF THE MOGHRABI SUFRAH. ABANDON HOPE, ALL YE WHO LINGER HERE!

The name "Moghrabi Sufrah," incidentally, had been rudely scratched out, and another name had been roughly carved above it.

That name was, "Zazamanc the Archimage."

Gaglioffo had been snatching forty winks behind the vampires' cage, when suddenly roused to wakefulness by the simple expedient of being kicked several times in the ribs and belly by a long-nailed and bony foot, which, of course, belonged to his master.

"They are here!" cried Zazamanc exultantly, his eyes glowing like feral lamps. "Rouse yourself, you slothful worm, and prepare to assist me!"

Groaning his prayers to Mahoum and Termagant, to say nothing of the ineffable Golfarin, the Paynim crawled to his feet, and went limping after his master, who proceeded through the winding ways of the cavern with rapid stride.

XXIV

WALKING CADAVERS

Mandricardo tested the sheer wall of rock, prodding at it with his sword, while the Amazon girl poked it here and there with her metal javelin, but they found no mode of entry.

"It probably works by wizardry," said Arimaspia, and the others agreed that she was doubtless correct in her assumption. Which still left them with the question of how to get inside.

Now Kesrick, as has been stated before, was fortunate enough to have enjoyed the benefits of an excellent education, and had read very much history. Since all else had failed, he now stepped forth to try his luck. Lifting his arms in a gesture of stern command, he cried in a great voice—

"OPEN, O SESAME!"

Before the last echoes of his voice had died, the portal yawned open before them. Arimaspia clasped her hands together between her white and lovely breasts, admiringly.

"Sometimes it works, sometimes it doesn't," murmured the Frankish knight with a modest smile.

They regarded the black and yawning mouth of the cavern, armed as it was with those fanglike stalactites and stalagmites, and the prospect did not look very hospitable. But before they had gathered their courage to enter, a horde of shambling, lurching figures appeared in the vestibule, before the very sight of which the Scythian Princess withdrew shudderingly on faltering steps, and even Sir Mandricardo paled and muttered, "Oh, I say, this *is* a bit much, what?"

For the staggering horde were composed of rotting cadavers and desiccated mummies, all animated, of course, by the vile necromancy of the Egyptian wizard. All were in advanced stages of decomposition, and some were little more than stalking skeletons, but in the eyes, or sockets, of each gleamed a furtive spark of red light that suggested sentience, and a lethal purposefulness as they came shambling, stumbling, lurching out into the clear light of day.

As there was nothing else to do but stand and fight these zombies, the knights and the Amazon girl unlimbered sword, spear and buckler, and entered into the grisly fray . . . although, I have no doubt, that one question flickered uneasily through the minds of them all, and that was: *how do you kill something that is already dead?*

Hewing lustily, and trying to ignore the stench which enveloped them and the buzzing cloud of gnats and carrion flies that hovered about the weirdly animated cadavers, they began chopping off arms and slicing off heads. None of which seemed to do the slightest good, for not only were their ghastly adversaries thoroughly insensible to pain, but they did not particularly seem to miss a lopped-off limb.

Kesrick took a swipe with his enchanted sword at one of the cadavers, neatly taking off its head; nevertheless, this decapitation did not even slow the creature down. It continued to advance upon him with clutching hands outspread, for all the world as if it could see him still.

Callipygia speared a few through gaunt chest or sunken belly with her Amazonian javelin, but, while this made them stagger back a foot or two, they continued to press upon her with grim purpose.

Only Arimaspia was naked of weaponry, even as she was of raiment, but the plucky Princess determinedly resolved not to stand idly by while her beloved and their friends fought and fell. Seizing up a hefty rock from the sands, she staggered to where one of the skeletons had circled around behind the Frank and brained it with the small boulder.

That is, if it had possessed any brains, the blow would have done the trick; as things turned out, while the bony skull shattered like an eggshell, the bony thing remained undeterred.

"Oh, dear!" she wailed, tossing back her long golden hair over her bare white shoulders, as the skeleton with the shattered skull reached out with bony claws to clutch Kesrick's throat from behind, while he was too busy holding at bay three cadavers to even so much as notice this latest menace.

Then she lifted the rock again and brought it down sharply in two blows upon the arm-bones of the skeleton. They snapped off like dry sticks underfoot, and the skeleton stood there for a moment as if nonplused, for without arms or hands it obviously was unable to clutch.

Arimaspia brightened.

"Cut off their arms!" she cried to her companions, "and they will not be able to harm you!"

"Jolly good idea, what?" puffed Sir Mandricardo, whereupon the Tartar knight ceased trying to inflict wounds upon the torso of his adversary, but, instead, employed his glittering blade to disarming the creature, so to speak.

The cadaver paused, even as Arimaspia's skeleton had done, and stood there swaying puzzledly for a moment, as if trying with slow and sluggish wits to figure out a way to do harm to the knight.

Then Mandricardo cut off both of its legs, and the armless and legless torso fell to the ground, unable to do more than merely wriggle.

"Good show, I say!" exulted the Tartar. Callipygia and Sir Kesrick wasted no time in adopting the mode of battle suggested by the Scythian Princess, and in less time than it would take to tell the tale, the victorious four stood, puffing and wheezing, surrounded by dismembered torsos and bodiless limbs, which were as unable to do them hurt or harm as they were unable to any further impede their progress into the cavern.

They warmly congratulated the Scythian Princess for her quick thinking, and she blushed and giggled under their praise. Then, gingerly stepping over wriggling torsos and flopping arms and legs, they advanced into the black mouth of the fanged cavern, leading their two steeds by the reins. Just inside the tunnel, they tethered the Hippogriff and Bayardetto to a stone stalagmite, and went forward cautiously into utter darkness.

Neither Brigadore nor Bayardetto liked the place much, and nickered and neighed uncomfortably, but finally grew quiet when they realized their riders were not at once going to return, and the two began nibbling distastefully at some mouldy straw which lay amid the filthy garbage.

They found all within the black tunnel the same as Gaglioffo had discovered, so I will not bother to repeat the description. Icy water dripped on them from the arched roof; slimy puddles and patches of fungi squished underfoot; rats as big as tabby-cats fled squeaking from their steps; bats flapped and whistled shrilly in the gloom; ugly fat toads hopped away to hide among the filth.

Alert and vigilant and wary, they progressed to the end of the tunnel, where the Wyverns in their stable hissed angrily at them through the iron bars.

Mandricardo peered around him in the gloom, for the human arms which sprouted from the wall held unlit torches, and the darkness was relieved only by glowing patches of phosphorescent mold. He shivered as a few droplets of icy, slimy water went trickling down the back of his neck.

"I say, dismal sort of place, what?" he muttered uneasily. They agreed with him, gazing around at the grim and somber surroundings.

Beyond the iron-barred cage which served the Egyptian wizard as a stable for his team of Wyverns, the tunnel opened out into a vast domed rotunda. Against the rugged walls were stacked heaps of broken and moldering furniture, empty boxes, bales and barrels, and a number of obsolete or, at least, seldom-used idols. These had grimacing faces of unparalleled hideousness, and generally bore several arms whose hands held or brandished swords, flowers, skulls, carven flames, and such-like symbolic emblems. Each of these was more ghastly looking than the one before it.

Arimaspia paused before one such, which had a bloated and corpulent body of verdigris-eaten brass. Scaly shoulders supported nine heads which grew one atop the other, and each head was smaller than the one beneath it, until by the time you got to the ninth and last head, it was mostly eye.

"What perfectly vile taste in sculpture!" said the Scythian Princess, disgustedly.

"Here's something over here," called Kesrick, who had been prowling about the cavern. He had found a flight of black marble stairs which led to a tall narrow opening . . .

With Kesrick leading the way, they climbed this stair and entered a long hall which was lit only by pits of burning sulfur. They glanced about, noticing the weird hangings and the throne-chair that earlier Gaglioffo had observed, but the room hall seemed untenanted.

"Blighter's got to be *somewhere*, you know!" puffed the Tartar knight, staring about.

"Let's search it to the far end, behind the chair," suggested the Frank, and the two knights entered the great hall, with Callipygia, and Arimaspia, following at their heels.

No sooner had all of them entered the hall, than suddenly

and without warning a great slab of rusty iron fell clanging to block the entrance, like a barbican-gate, and they saw none other than Gaglioffo, looking frightened, apologetic and guilty all at the same time, standing by the windlass. The Paynim had been concealed behind a tapestry, stationed there on orders of Zazamanc, to release the iron barrier once all were within.

They turned to confront him, but the Paynim displayed sooty hands innocent of weapons. Then, as the harsh and clanging echoes which the falling of the iron door had awakened, ebbed, a grating and malicious laughter came to their ears.

Again they turned, to see the tall, gaunt, menacing form of the Egyptian wizard melting into being out of empty air, standing before his throne, his brow wreathed with hissing vipers, his eyes gloating down at them with evil glee.

"Welcome to my subterranean palace," he leered in a cold, suave voice. "As your host, dear but uninvited guests, I hope that you enjoy your stay, for these will be the last sights that ever you look upon in this life!"

XXV

THE MAGIC POMMEL-STONE

Zazamanc, whom Arimaspia, Mandricardo, and Callipygia had never before seen, was tall and gaunt, with hunched, bony shoulders and long arms, whose hands were armed with clawlike nails. He had a hooked beard, dyed vermillion, and a bony, sallow face, with scowling black brows and burning, evil eyes. On this occasion, he wore a long tight gown of snaky-green, bound at his thin waist with a girdle woven of strands of human skin. Talismanic rings flashed and glowed on his fingers, and small idols and periapts of agate, carved pearl, and blue or yellow paste were slung about his scrawny neck on strands of copper wire or upon leathern thongs. His starched Egyptian headdress was bound about the brows, as I have said, with a wreath of living vipers.

He looked altogether menacing and potent in his wizardly powers. But Kesrick faced him boldly, having come this far for just this confrontation.

"Dastardly villain," declared Kesrick in ringing tones, "you have persecuted and pursued me for reasons best known to yourself! Now are we come to the final confrontation, wherefrom either you or I will emerge the victor. You have no genii to assist you now, and all of your walking cadavers lie dismembered upon the sands before your stony door; there is naught but the whimpering and treacherous Gaglioffo to stand by your side—"

"Take care, young fool of a Frank," purred the Egyptian in silken tones. "Your small and mortal mind cannot conceive of the powerful supernatural aides that I can freely summon to my defense with a snap of the fingers."

"I care not a jot for them," said Kesrick boldly, "for right is on my side, and in this history, I am the hero and you the villain. Right will ever triumph over might!"

"Oh, I say!" breathed Sir Mandricardo fervently. "Jolly good, what?"

"Cunningly have I lured you here to mine subterraneous abode," said Zazamanc, "where I sit enthroned amid the might of my wizardly powers, and where you, rash and foolish intruder, are helpless to oppose me. True, you won through the tomb-herd that I dispatched to ward my portals, but that was brute strength alone, against animated corpses, whereas now you face, in the very citadel and fortress of his powers, a cunning and wise adversary, armed with every magical weapon which human ingenuity has ever devised, and your chances of survival, and the chances of those hapless dupes who have stupidly accompanied you here, are minuscule, to say the least!"

"You speak boldly," declared Kesrick, the sword Dastagerd naked in his capable hand, "but actions speak louder than words, as the poet says: strike, then, and have done—or I will come to where you stand, and seize you by the beard, and cut off your wicked head, putting an end once and for all, to your unparalleled villainies!"

And, with that, he stepped forward boldly, but Zazamanc stayed him with a lifted hand, whose palm bore like a cup a glowing ball of icy white fire.

"I could slay you where you stand, dog of a Frank," hissed the Egyptian wizard, "in any number of ways. I could reduce you to a cinder in a globe of slowly closing flame, or smite you with a thunderbolt, or reduce you to ashes, dust or powder in an instant. But it pleases me to ever have your very image and likeness near me, so that I can gloat over it as I enjoy the innumerable centuries of life yet left to me. Therefore, shall I turn you into a marble statue—"

And with this, he hurled directly at the young knight the seething globe of white fire he held in one cupped palm.

And Kesrick, his shield forgotten, instinctively held up before his face the pommel of Dastagerd.

Now Dastagerd was the Sword of Undoings; and the enchanted magic pommel-stone, as has been explained, possesses the power to repel and to reflect back upon the enchanter any evil spell or enchantment directed at him who bears in his hand the famous Sword of Undoings.

Thus did the Egyptian wizard (who had, in his hatred and fury, momentarily forgotten that the pommel-stone had been replaced in the enchanted sword) shriek aloud in unbelieving horror and in despair, as he felt his feet, and calves, and legs freeze into solid marble.

Looking fearfully down, he saw the white tide advance up his lower extremities like a chilling frost. To the knees, then to the thigh, then to hip and belly, the transformation advanced, while the four adventurers looked on staring with relief and amazement.

With a croak of unbelieving horror, Zazamanc called upon Ashtoreth, upon Asmodeus, and upon Abraxas, but to no avail, for such was the potency of the pommel-stone of Dastagerd, the Sword of Undoings, which proved, even as the stars which had reigned at his nativity had warned Zazamanc, to be his Undoing.

In a moment, his breast had turned to marble, and then his throat, and he was beyond speech, was the wizard.

They stood as if stunned, for only a glistening statue of pure white marble stood upon the steps which led to the throne.

And Zazamanc was no more.

Gaglioffo threw himself at their feet, wriggling upon his belly and trying to kiss their boots, but they spurned him, and he crept into a corner and huddled there, weeping miserably—and not because of the curious doom which had befallen his wicked master, but because of the sudden and cruel punishment which the Paynim feared would fall upon him next.

Arimaspia threw herself upon Kesrick's bosom, sobbing with happiness, and they embraced and kissed. In much the same mood, the Tartar seized the astounded Amazon girl in his arms and sealed her red lips with a not-entirely-unwelcome kiss. For the quest was over and done, the villain destroyed, and joy and happiness lay ahead for the victors.

After these brief but affectionate embraces, there was still work to do. With Gaglioffo leading them, they thoroughly explored and ransacked every crypt and corner of the subterranean palace, but found no living prisoners to set free, unless you care to count the werewolf. They actually did free the werewolf, who scampered off howling into the wilderness, because they thought him nothing more than merely a beast, nor did Gaglioffo care to disabuse them of the notion.

"We cannot leave these pitiful creatures chained up to starve," declared Arimaspia, viewing the captive monsters immured in the wizard's menagerie. Moved by her own humanitarian pleadings, Kesrick and Mandricardo and Callipygia, however unwillingly, set each and every monster free to pursue his or her or its own fate in the wilderness.

These things being accomplished, they returned to the outer tunnel again, relieved to discover that the door still stood open and that the escaping monstrosities had not bothered to molest their steeds, which neighed and nickered happily, at the sight of their humans emerging whole and unscathed from the black bowels of the underground castle.

"If only your friend, the wise sorcerer, were here to see with what ease, and remarkable finality, we disposed of the Egyptian!" sighed Arimaspia, leaning upon the strong arm of her hero, as they left the noisome caverns.

"Jolly right, what?" Sir Mandricardo chimed in heartily. "Or Dame Whatzername, dash it all, you know, your Fairy Godmother!"

Kesrick nodded, saying nothing; he had a presentiment that, at that very instant of time, both Pteron of Taprobane and Pirouetta, the Fairy of the Fountain, were observing with satisfaction the triumphant conclusion of their adventures, through this or that magic crystal, or whatever.

And he was, of course, quite right.

Leading their steeds out into the sands beyond the yawning portal (which closed, quite properly, when Kesrick bade it to "Close, O Sesame!"), they looked about them at the luminous lavender skies of evening.

"As for the Princess and myself, we shall depart at once for Dragonrouge and home," said Kesrick, "to set all things aright, and to hallow our nuptials in the village chapel. But what of yourself, my Tartar friend, and of the Princess of the Amazons?"

"Well, old boy," said Mandricardo cheerfully, "if all's agreeable to you, we would fain accompany you to the true conclusion of your quest, and, mayhap (for who can say, what, and wonders still *do* happen), Madame Callipygia and myself may well join you at the jolly old altar in a double ceremony, eh?"

"I could pray for nothing more splendid," declared Kesrick, smiling, and clasping the hand of his friend.

"But what of the poor little Paynim?" inquired Arimaspia, a bit anxiously, peering about. But Gaglioffo was nowhere to be espied; he had slunk away while their attentions were diverted by their farewells, and had vanished from sight.

"Leave the beggar to his own devices," sniffed the Tartar

knight. "He has been nothing but a thorn in our foot and a stitch in our side from the beginning."

And so they were forced to abandon the bow-legged little Paynim to whatever dooms or fates Providence had planned for him, which were doubtless to prove no more or less than he had already, and that richly, deserved.

And so we take leave of our heroes and heroines, as they ride forth from the subterranean palace of the vanquished wizard, and direct their travels toward the World's West, toward the old House of Dragonrouge, and to whatever blissful times or future adventures Terra Magica, and the gods who rule Terra Magica, have in store for them.

The perils can be no more direful than were those they have already surpassed, and the happiness that awaits them, surely, is happiness beyond their several experiences.

In the manner that such histories conclude, then, let us assume that:

They all lived happily ever after.

The Notes to KESRICK

While the histories of the sword Dastagerd, the knight Kesrick, the Princess Arimaspia, and the sorcerer Pteron, have hitherto gone unchronicled, most of the other people, places and things mentioned in this book have not gone unrecorded. Therefore, I append these notes for the use of my readers, in order to avoid making them waste their own time trying to find my sources.

CHAPTER I

Dedaim tree. Gustave Flaubert mentioned this tree, which grew near Babylon and which bore as fruit severed human heads, in his delicious fantasy extravaganza, *The Temptations of St. Anthony.*

Crysaor. Vulcan made this sword for Jupiter to use in his war against the Titans, at least according to Edmund Spenser in his Elizabethan allegorical epic, *The Faerie Queene.*

Dietrich. The history of Dietrich of Berne and of the sword Nagelring is given in the old German romances; Dastagerd, however, is not mentioned.

Huon. He was a mortal paladin of Bordeaux in the Carolingian romances, who became High King of All Faerie upon the death of King Oberon. See the French romance, *Huon of Bordeaux.*

Guyon. Sir Guyon was one of the knights whose adventures are related in *The Faerie Queene.*

Taprobane. For some reason, the island nation just south of India has gone by an amazing variety of names throughout its long history. Among these are Serendib, Taprobane, Ceylon, and—most recently—Sri Lanka. The famous Sindbad of Bassorah visited it on one of his voyages.

CHAPTER II

Mantichore. My description of this fabulous beast is drawn from Flaubert's *St. Anthony.*

Tarandus. I have hitherto been unable to discover this beast in any of the older authors of Unnatural History, but Cabell describes him in his fine fantasy novel, *The High Place,* first published in 1923.

Ouranabad. A monstrous winged Hydra, mentioned by William Beckford in his remarkable novel, *Vathek,* written either in 1781 or 1782 (the authorities differ).

Melusinae. It was the medieval writer Paracelsus who assigned to the Four Elements their respective symbolic Geniuses, and the Malusinae were those designated in his system to represent water. The name comes from a celebrated mermaid in old German stories. Incidentally, Taprobane (or Serendib, or Ceylon, or whatever you wish to call it) was famous from of old for its mermaids. Seven of the species were reportedly netted by native fishermen in 1560, as the testimony of Jesuit scholars demonstrates, in the *Historia de la Compagnie de Jesus*; but long before there were any Jesuits, the Greek geographer Megasthenes wrote that mermaids were often seen off the waters of Taprobane.

The history of the ring Draupnir, and of the Dwarves Brokk and Sindri, are given in the Norse Myths.

Erythraean Sea. This was the name by which the ancient Greek geographers called the Indian Ocean.

CHAPTER III

Shadukiam. In the Arabian Nights, the rosy-domed city of the Genii.

Soham. A monster out of Islamic legend, mentioned and described in Beckford's *Vathek.*

Tregelaphus. A beast also described in *Vathek.* You really must read it: it has to be the best novel that anyone in all of the world ever wrote in three days.

Catoblepas. This is one of the eight beasts chained before the gates of King Helmas' castle, in Cabell's *The High Place.*

The Askar. In ancient rabbinical lore, a monstrous python which once scared the dickens out of Moses. What Pteron was doing with it chained in his front yard, I have no idea.

Syl. Yet another creature described in *Vathek*.

Senmurv. The dog-headed, barking eagles of Persian folklore.

Senad. This is another of the fabulous beasts described by Flaubert in his *St. Anthony*.

Atlantes. The history of this famous magician is given in the Italian romantic epic, the *Orlando Furioso*. He really did breed Hippogriffs.

Pausengi. Both this tree and the Upas were described by Willy Ley in his book, *Salamanders and Other Wonders*.

Baaras roots. Also depicted in Flaubert's extravaganza.

Tingaribinus. I doubt very much if this color is actually lost; probably the classical writers who referred to it in such terms were thinking of some dye whose secret composition had been forgotten. But the notion of a "lost color" so excited my imagination, that I will take it to mean what it says.

The Nag-Kanya are indeed fish-tailed maidens in Hindu myth. There would seem to be quite a few different varieties of mermaid, such as these and the Melusinae mentioned earlier, and also the Margyr, with their webbed hands, horrible faces, double chins, and fishy tails, who are only sighted in the seas around Greenland.

Phoenix. This remarkable and very long-lived fowl is too well known in story to deserve an explanatory note here. But this particular phoenix, in background and description, happens to be the very same one who has an important role in Voltaire's charming romance, *The Princess of Babylon*.

Imlac. The national poet of the Ethiopians, according to Samuel Johnson in his famous novella, *Rasselas*.

Epigenes Rhodius, et al. These various classical authors were unfortunate in that all of their works have been completely lost. We know of them only through mentions in Pliny and other extant scholars of antiquity. It would seem that the literary works lost in Terra Cognita are alive and being well-read in Terra Magica.

Axieros, et al. These are among the Forgotten Gods; Axieros was one of the three gods of Samothrace, while Taranis was a storm god worshipped by the Celts; Pthah, of course, was the creator god of the ancient Egyptians.

Nectanebus. Historically, the last true Pharaoh of Egypt, as after him came the Macedonian and Roman conquests; in the legendary history of Alexander the Great, he was a mighty magician as well as Pharaoh.

CHAPTER IV

Hydrargyrum. The name by which alchemists refer to an imaginary metal, "fixed quicksilver."

Yale. In the medieval bestiaries, a fabulous animal akin to elk or reindeer.

Chalibon. In Flaubert's *St. Anthony,* a precious wine of which only the Assyrian kings might drink.

Orichalc. In Plato, a metal used by the Atlanteans, otherwise unknown.

Zazamanc. For the history of this Egyptian wizard, see the second tale in the "Tales of the Magicians" section, in Flinders Petrie's *Egyptian Tales,* first published in London in 1895.

Sosorthos and Sesostris. The names by which the Greek historians knew the Pharaohs Zoser and Senusert III.

Tarquinius. One of the several imaginary Emperors of Rome who appears in an old and marvelous collection of wonder tales called the *Gesta Romanorum.*

Zantipher Magnus. An imaginary classical authority cited by James Branch Cabell's character Jurgen in the famous novel of the same name.

Fulgentius. Another imaginary Emperor from the *Gesta Romanorum*; or, if not actually imaginary, at least one who never lorded it over Rome here in Terra Cognita, the Lands We Know.

Domdaniel. In medieval times it was thought that magicians studied at this submaritime university off Tunis. See Burton's notes to his translation of the *Arabian Nights.*

Soliman Djinn-ben Djinn, the Pre-Adamite Kings, and Kaf. All are drawn from Islamic folklore; see the Notes to William Beckford's *Vathek* for more information.

Posidippus. A classical dramatist whose works are entirely lost.

Zorobasius and Ptolemopiters. Two imaginary classical writers invented by Chloris to confound Jurgen; she was evidently as weary as Kesrick with citations of classical authorities she had never heard of. And, incidentally, Jurgen pretended to be familiar with their works, even as Pteron does in this scene.

CHAPTER V

Annals of the Genii. This book is mentioned by Beckford in the second tale in his *Episodes of Vathek*, a collection of tales which were not included in the novel.

The Mandiran. This spell is discussed by the eighteenth-century French writer, Augustin-Paradis de Moncrief, in his fantasy tale, "Rival Souls." Incidentally, the same Prince Sikander of Ballasor from whom Pteron had the secret is the villain of that story.

Rhiphaeans. The classical geographers believed these mountains to exist in the most northerly parts of Asia, between Scythia and Hyperborea. Hyperborea was an imaginary land dreamed up by Greek writers such as Pindar, but Scythia existed in history and occupied parts of what is now the Soviet Union.

Efreet. In Islamic legend, the Genii are divided into three races or nations: the Marids, the Efreets, and the Jan. See Burton's notes to the *Arabian Nights.*

Magic Horse. For the history of this remarkable equine, see the "Tale of the Magic Horse" in the *Arabian Nights.*

Imgur-Bel. This is the actual name of the Great Wall of Babylon.

Nimrod. A legendary king who supposedly ruled before the Flood, and who built the Tower of Babel (that is, the great ziggurat of Babylon).

Gog and Magog. According to the fabulous history of Alexander, this wall was built to keep the two savage peoples from overrunning the civilized world. In other versions of the history, they are two giants.

Hippogriff. The members of this species were the results of a chance mating between mares and griffons; these are not actually fabulous creatures, but were invented by the Italian romancer Ariosto, and first appeared in his *Orlando Furioso.*

Brigadore. The name means "Bridle of Gold," and it was the name of Sir Guyon's steed in *The Faerie Queene*, although I have a strong hunch that Spenser borrowed it from "Brigliadoro," the name of the steed of Orlando, otherwise known as Roland, in the Carolingian romances.

Aglibol, et al. Three more of the Forgotten Gods. It would seem that our Pteron somewhat fancied the more obscure and obsolete mythologies. Aglibol was the moon god of Palmyra, and Tarku a divinity worshipped in Asia Minor, and, as for Centeotl, she was the earth-goddess of the Aztecs.

CHAPTER VI

Thamimasadas. Appropriately (given the scene), the Scythian sea god; also, given the lineage of the Princess, the god by which only those of the Scythian Blood Royal might swear or to whom they prayed.

Rogero, etc. The history of the paladin Rogero, of Princess Angelica of Cathay, and of the monstrous Orc, may be found in the *Orlando Furioso.*

Perseus and Andromeda. They appear, of course, in the Greek Myths. See Bullfinch's *Mythology.*

Bellerophon. The story of Bellerophon and the Chimera comes also from the Greek myths. Bellerophon, incidentally, was not mounted on a flying steed at the time of his famous duel with the hybrid monster, but was wearing winged sandals loaned to him by Mercury.

Rosmarin. An huge sea-monster described in the medieval bestiaries as resembling a gigantic walrus or sea lion.

Octamasadas, etc. A Scythian king of that name died in the times of Herodotus, so I presume he was the first of that name. A Queen Thomyris of Scythia is mentioned in one of the poems of Swinburne. Arimaspia's name may derive from one of the older Scythian tribes, the Arimaspi, who lived at that time on the borders of Cathay; I presume they eventually conquered Scythia and founded a royal dynasty.

Quinapalus. A classical authority known only to us from his being mentioned in Shakespeare's comedy, *Twelfth Night.*

CHAPTER VII

Abaris. This Hyperborean magician is mentioned by some of the ancient Greek writers, but little of his story has survived.

Arthame. A special sort of knife used in magical ceremonies.

Aipolos, et al. Yet more of the Forgotten Gods; Aipolos was one of the gods worshipped by the Phrygians; Merodach was the Babylonian sun god from whom the Kings of Babylon claimed descent; and Tuisco was worshipped by the ancient Teutons.

Zaqqum, and Zamzam. Islamic oaths; see Burton's notes to his *Arabian Nights.*

Mahoum. According to François Rabelais, in his *Gargantua and Pantagruel*, suchlike Paynims as Moors and Saracens swear by Mahoum, and who am I to dispute him?

CHAPTER VIII

Potion, etc. This is the identical spell used by the wicked witch, old Mombi, to remove the transformation she had earlier placed upon the Princess Ozma, in L. Frank Baum's beloved childrens' classic, *The Land of Oz*, first published in 1904 as a sequel to the immortal *Wizard*, and the first of more than forty Oz books by various writers. Mr. Baum knows much more about magic than I do (in every sense of the term), so I yield happily to his authority on rites of disenchantment.

Golfarin. Another idol worshipped, or at least sworn by, among the Paynims in Rabelais.

Termagant. A Paynim goddess mentioned in Sir John de Mandeville.

CHAPTER IX

Phrygia, Paphlagonia, etc. These are ancient countries of Asia, long since invaded, conquered, absorbed and forgotten, and concerning which very little is known.

Soccotra. An Oriental country or island mentioned in the old travelers' tales, such as the *Travels and Voyages* of the famous Sir John de Mandeville.

Agathodaemon, et al. Forgotten gods, Agathodaemon was the serpent-god of the Phoenicians, while Zababa was the vulture-headed god of the Babylonians. As for Latobius, he was the war god of the Gauls.

CHAPTER X

Low, brutish cunning. As shall later be made explicit, the Efreet was one of the cronies or confederates of the Egyptian Wizard, Zazamanc, and I suspect the Garden of Jewels was his idea.

Melcarth. The Carthaginian Hercules.

St. George, etc. For this story you will have to consult an old Elizabethan chapbook, called *The Seven Champions of Christendom*, or a more recent retelling.

Well named. The word for "blue" in Arabic is " 'azraq."

Kashkash. The Genie here swears by the very oldest of all the Genii.

CHAPTER XI

Acoran, et al. Acoran was a divinity worshipped by the Canary Islanders; Qat was the creator-god of the Melanesians, and Abraxas one of the gods worshipped by the heretical Gnostics.

Calphurnius Bassus, Alcofribas Nasier. The first of these is an imaginary authority mentioned in Rabelais, while the second—whose name, you will notice, is an anagram of "François Rabelais"—is the pretended author of *Gargantua and Pantagruel.*

CHAPTER XII

Pantharb. A "fiery red magnetic jewel" owned by the Hindoo magician, Iarchas, who showed it to Appolonius according to the Roman biographer, Philostratus in his *Life of Appolonius of Tyana.*

Deggial. The future "Antichrist" of the Mussulmans.

Ampharool. The Genie who can teach the secret of flying

to men, according to a medieval grimoire called *The Book of Power*.

Aptly named. "Gaglioffo" is an Italian name which may be translated as "scoundrel."

CHAPTER XIII

Sauromatia. The Scythian capital was left unnamed by those classical historians and geographers who discussed the nation, so I have taken the liberty of naming it after one of the royal tribes of Scythia, the Sauromatae, who dwelt upon the banks of the Tanais.

Antipodes. Lands presumed by the ancient geographers to exist in the extremest south, beyond the Ocean River.

Getiafrose. The Queen of All Genii, according to Burton's *Arabian Nights.*

CHAPTER XIV

Jarhibol and Acoran. More of the Forgotten Gods: the first was the sun god of ancient Palmyra, the second a divinity worshipped in the Canary Islands.

Kahmurath, et al. These are the ancient mythological Kings of Persia, as given in the *Shah-Namah.*

CHAPTER XV

Mandricardo. The history of this Tartar knight, and of his father, King Agricane, can be found in the Italian verse romance, *Orlando Furioso,* or any of its several retellings.

The Wandering Garden. Its real name was the Bower of Bliss, and the enchantress Acrasia invented it to entrap wandering knights, whom she then seduced, turning them into pine trees or something later on, when she got bored with them. You can read all about it in Spenser's *Faerie Queene.* He seemed to think it was on an island, but maybe there were a couple of them.

Antonius Diogenes. An ancient writer whose works have been thoroughly lost; all we know about him was that he wrote about Ultima Thule.

Zipangu. A name for Japan on some of the older European maps.

CHAPTER XVI

Pirouetta. The history of this powerful Fairy seems to have hitherto gone unchronicled, but she bears a distinct resemblance to some of the Fairy Godmothers described in the wittier of the French fairy tales of Perrault and Madame d'Aulnoy.

Meropis. An imaginary continent beyond the Western Sea. No, it was not the Americas.

Bayardetto. Bayard was the name of the famous horse ridden by Amadis of Gaul, in the Portuguese romance of the same name. "Bayardetto" means "Little Bayard," and Mandricardo probably gave his steed this affectionate name in remembrance of the more famous charger.

CHAPTER XVII

Adamant. The old poets and writers mention this metal as if it really existed, which it does not, at least here in Terra Cognita. The diamond, strongest of all gems, is named after it.

Mother Gothel. According to the Brothers Grimm, this was the name of the witch who locked up Rapunzel in that tower.

Hut on Chicken Legs. This sounds very much to me like Izbushka, the hut of the witch Baba Yaga in the Russian fairy tales.

St. Adauras. In Rabelais, the patron of those who deserve hanging; no one of this name appears on the Calendar of Saints in Terra Cognita, however.

CHAPTER XVIII

Izbushkha. I was right, then: this *was* the hut on chicken legs formerly owned by Baba Yaga.

Water. Witches are notoriously difficult to slay, but as L. Frank Baum reminds us, in *The Wizard of Oz*, they dissolve when soaked in fresh water (which was how Dorothy destroyed the Wicked Witch of the West in that book, you will remember, when she accidentally threw a pail of water on her). Mr. Baum knew a lot more than I do about witches, and I am willing to accept his authority on this point.

CHAPTER XIX

Amadis. Here in Terra Cognita, he is merely the hero of a celebrated prose romance of considerable length and of great, but now outdated, popularity. In Terra Magica, he is a figure of history, it would seem, otherwise the townsfolk would hardly have erected a statue to him in the town square.

Gluckstein. A town in the kingdom of Pantouflia; both it and the river Gluckthal are mentioned in Andrew Lang's delightful children's fantasy about Pantouflia (the first of three such), *Prince Prigio.*

Orn. A small country in Frank Stockton's fairy tale, "The Bee-Man of Orn."

CHAPTER XX

Eridanus. An ancient name for the river Po.

Amazonia. An imaginary country in Asia, according to the Greeks, inhabited by women warriors.

CHAPTER XXI

Sesame. The same magic phrase which Ali Baba heard used by the leader of the Forty Thieves, to open the stone portals of their treasure-cave, in the *Arabian Nights.* Zazamanc does not seem to have been very original in his choice of "key" words.

Lamussa, et al. These are various mythological or legendary creatures mentioned in Flaubert and elsewhere, as in Cabell's *The High Place.* Only the Hippocamp, or seahorse, is of classical origin. The Myrmicolion, one of the most interesting of the hybrids, was half lion and half gigantic red ant.

Alifanfaron, et al. The first of these was the Emperor of Serendib, in *Don Quixote.* Fayoles was the fourth king of Numidia, according to Rabelais. Brandabarbaran also is mentioned in Cervantes.

Tarniel. An angel of Mercury who is most powerful in the third hour of Wednesdays, and, according to the *Ozar Midrashim* II, 316, a guardian of the gates of the East Wind. You probably think I am making most of this up, don't you?

Hippolyta, et al. Amazonian queens who appear in various of the Greek myths and epics. Hippolyta lived in the age of Hercules, while Penthesilaea fought at the final battles against Troy. I forget who Kaydessa was.

Megamastaia. The name is fair Greek for "Big Breasts."

Aptly named. "Callipygia" is also fair Greek for "Beautiful Buttocks."

CHAPTER XXII

River Cinyps, etc. Most of these are countries or tribes believed to inhabit the desert regions of Africa, and are mentioned in Pliny's description of that part of the world, or in the *Geography* of Claudius Ptolemy.

Sadhuzag. A monster described in Flaubert's *Temptations of Saint Anthony.*

Pastinaca. The habits and person of this fetid and gigantic weasel are given in the medieval bestiaries.

The Moghrab. In Islamic legend, and in the *Arabian*

Nights, a desolate region in Mauretania which was notorious for being the residence of evil magicians and wicked spirits.

CHAPTER XXIII

Piast. An enormous, lake-dwelling serpent in Irish legends.

Phalmant. The appearance and habits of this curious beast Phalmant are given in Flaubert's *St. Anthony*, and I have yet to discover the creature mentioned anywhere else.

Moghrabi Sufrah. This is no other than Aladdin's uncle, the African magician; his proper name is not given in the tale, however, but comes from the biographer Schwab, in his admirable *Imaginary Lives.*

CHAPTER XXIV

Necromancy. This is one of the Black Arts by which cadavers or skeletons could temporarily be animated by recalling back to their former abode those spirits which had once inhabited them; this was for the principal purpose of divining the future. Zazamanc seems to have used them after the manner of zombies, as slaves or servants.

Nine heads. This was an effigy of the demon Phul, by the way. You will find him in most of the better compendiums of demonology.

CHAPTER XXV

Undoings. Obviously, Dastagerd was called the "Sword of Undoings" because it could undo, and even reflect backwards, any spell hurled against him who bore it. A useful thing to have with you, if you happen to be a hero in a magical adventure, you will agree.

Ashtoreth, etc. Dukes and Princes of Hell, according to the demonologists. Abraxas was a Gnostic demiurge.

A WORD OF APPRECIATION

I am indebted to three of my friends in The Trap Door Spiders for certain of the linguistic puns which occur in this book, and would like to thank them now for adding to the richness and wit of this true and veritable History: to Dr. L. Sprague de Camp, for supplying me with the names of the Efreet and his brother in Arabic; to Dr. Gilbert Cant for assisting me with the Greek names of the Amazon queen and her daughter; and to Dr. Jean LeCorbeiller for giving me the scrap of Latin quoted in Chapter IV. Good men all!